Ballet Academy

EDENDERRY

1 0 DEC 2021

WITHDRAWN

D1368876

Find out more about the characters
and the Academy at:

www.piccadillypress.co.uk/balletacademy

The *Ballet Academy* series

Companion book:
The World of Ballet

Ballet Academy

Friends
Old and New

BEATRICE MASINI

Translation by Laura Watkinson

PICCADILLY PRESS • LONDON

First published in Great Britain in 2009
by Piccadilly Press Ltd,
5 Castle Road, London NW1 8PR
www.piccadillypress.co.uk

Text copyright © Beatrice Masini, 2005
English language translation © Laura Watkinson 2009
Translated from the original *Amici Vecchi e Nuovi*,
published by Edizioni EL, Trieste, Italy
www.edizioniel.com
Published by arrangement with Rights People, London

All rights reserved. No part of this publication may be reproduced,
stored in a retrieval system, or transmitted in any form or by
any means electronic, mechanical, photocopying, recording
or otherwise, without the prior permission
of the copyright owner.

The right of Beatrice Masini to be identified as Author of this work
has been asserted by her in accordance with
the Copyright, Designs and Patents Act, 1988.

A catalogue record for this book is available
from the British Library

ISBN: 978 1 84812 033 4

Printed in the UK by CPI Bookmarque, Croydon, CR0 4TD
Cover design by Patrick Knowles
Cover illustration by Sara Not

Chontae Uibh Fhaíl

Class: JF

Acc: 13,6104

Inv: 13 1137

€6·04

FSC

Mixed Sources
Product group from well-managed
forests and other controlled sources
www.fsc.org Cert no. TT-COC-002227
© 1996 Forest Stewardship Council

CHAPTER ONE

Missing
Madame Olenska

When Madame Olenska went back to Russia to visit her family in St Petersburg, everyone knew that although it was just a short trip, it would have a huge impact on the Academy. With the headmistress away, were the mice going to play? No, it wasn't quite as simple as that. Madame Olenska *was* the Academy, even more so than the elegant red and gold crest that appeared above the entrance to the school and theatre and was printed on all of the posters, school reports and certificates. No one could imagine what it would be like without her for a whole two months.

As they walked out one breaktime, Zoe deliberately hung back in the main corridor. Leda stopped to wait for her, but Zoe waved her on. She wanted to go very slowly past the door to Madame Olenska's office and peep inside. The door was closed, but Zoe couldn't make out the usual silhouette moving around behind the frosted glass. Instead there was just an empty space behind the desk.

The substitute teacher hadn't arrived yet, and no one even knew if it was going to be a man or a woman. Zoe was sure that the replacement was going to be some kind of vague, insignificant person, like substitutes always tend to be, who would disappear and be forgotten as soon as everything went back to normal. But she hoped that the new person was at least going to be a good teacher. Zoe enjoyed doing the barre exercises and central practice that Madame Olenska usually taught, and she didn't want to feel that she was just going through the motions. That would be such a waste of time – like when Madame Olenska had been ill. It had happened only once in six years, for two weeks. And that woman who had stood in for her . . . What was her name again? Oh yes, Mrs Meyer. That was it. She was so nervous that she made everyone else feel nervous too. Zoe guessed that she was frightened of children and that they made her feel uncomfortable. She didn't seem to know how to deal with them at all. She just kept on simpering 'daaarling' at them and she never told anyone off. Zoe remembered that when Madame Olenska returned, it took her over a month to get them all back in line, back to the disciplined ways in which she worked.

'You are full of faults,' she thundered at them. 'It's as though you've all caught fleas and I have to remove them, one by one!' What a nasty idea! But it had been so reassuring to hear her cane again, thumping up and down, boom boom, to the beat of your heart.

Without Madame Olenska around, they were all a little louder, particularly in the playground, and everyone was a bit more rowdy when they played games. This may also have been because it was nearly spring, even if it was still very cold.

Zoe caught up with the others, her hands thrust deep into the pockets of her quilted winter coat. In a moment of optimism, she'd left her hat inside, but her freezing ears told her that she'd made a mistake. Never mind. Roberto walked over, gave Zoe a smile, then reached inside her pocket to take her hand. Their fingers searched and found each other and then laced together. Their two hands fitted each other perfectly, and she felt a little warmer.

Lucas ran over to them, closely followed by Leda. 'Do you want to play dodgeball?' he asked. 'If you move around a bit, it warms you up. Better than just standing there with your teeth chattering.'

They reluctantly admitted that he was right. 'Okay then. Let's play,' said Leda. But everyone was still too cold, so they just stood there, looking at each other shivering, with vacant expressions on their faces. Some stubborn snow was still hanging around after the recent spell of bad weather. It had been quite extraordinary for March and the snow had paralysed the city for two whole days.

'The first thing that mountaineers lose when they're suffering from exposure is their big toes,' Leda announced in a gloomy voice. Everyone burst out laughing. Losing your big toes would be an absolute tragedy for a group of young dancers.

'You know the girl in *The Red Shoes*? That story by Hans Christian Andersen? She had both of her feet chopped off, just to get rid of the cursed shoes that made her dance and dance without ever stopping,' Paula added.

They all looked at each other and laughed again, together. There was a strange feeling of lightness in the air, something you could almost smell, something that you could breathe in. Spring? Maybe. Freedom? Perhaps.

Things felt odd again later when they had a study period instead of their usual barre lesson; no getting changed or tidying their hair really carefully – Madame Olenska wouldn't put up with a single stray hair escaping from the girls' buns. The class had been cancelled for that day and the next. The new teacher would arrive on Monday.

At the end of the day, Roberto wasn't waiting for Zoe as he usually did; he was having an extra English lesson. He could speak English well, but he still had some problems writing it, so he often had extra classes. Zoe headed outside, thinking about how everyone liked holidays, and that even severe Madame should be enjoying her time away from the Academy.

'Hey, Zoe!'

Leda ran to catch up with her and put a hand on her shoulder. 'Why didn't you wait for me?'

'Sorry,' said Zoe. 'I was miles away, thinking about stuff.'

'Stuff? You mean Roberto, don't you?' Leda giggled.

'Come on, don't be silly. I was just thinking about Madame Olenska.'

'Going away on holiday for two whole months,' mused Leda as they continued walking. 'Lucky her.'

'It must have been really tough for her when she left Russia all those years ago.'

'Lots of people left, didn't they? Because they hated the government there. Dad told me all about it when he gave me that poster of Nureyev.'

Zoe knew the poster she was talking about. It was

really dramatic, in black and white, and showed a dancer doing an elegant jump, with his feet together, tall, agile, strong. He was one of the greatest ballet dancers the world had ever seen.

They arrived at the bus stop, and as they waited for the bus, Zoe looked around. Even though it was a cold day, the sky was bright and blue. The world seemed to be newly painted.

'Why are you so worried about Madame Olenska?' asked Leda. 'I mean, it's a relief that she's not going to be here for a while, isn't it? I don't think you could find a stricter teacher anywhere, not on Mars or Jupiter or Saturn, not in all of the galaxies, not in the entire universe . . .'

Zoe started to speak, but the bus had finally arrived and her reply was lost in the hiss of the brakes and the swish of doors opening. Even if there was no stricter teacher in the entire known and unknown universe, Zoe wanted to explain to Leda that Madame Olenska meant a lot to her, even if she was sometimes so strict that she seemed quite mean. She wanted to say that Madame Olenska wasn't really that bad, that she was fair and that she always did what was right. Madame Olenska wanted each of them to do their best and she did everything she could to make that happen, even at the risk of seeming unpleasant.

Leda was Zoe's best friend and she'd listen to her and

maybe she'd understand, but then again, she might not. She might still insist on seeing Madame Olenska as an adult who was very different from them. But even though friends can have different opinions, Zoe decided to keep these thoughts to herself. It was too difficult to share exactly what she meant. And so she didn't reply, but just slid over to the seat by the window and looked out at the darkening sky.

CHAPTER TWO

A Special Monday

'Tonsillitis? Yeah, right. Sure it was. Have you ever heard of anyone having tonsillitis that lasts a month?' asked Paula. She needn't have said anything at all. Everybody knew that Alissa hadn't had tonsillitis for a month, that she'd had an eating disorder verging on anorexia. It was just an excuse for her having been away from school for so long.

'What does it matter to you? She's back now and that's the important thing, isn't it?' Zoe heard the words coming from her mouth and was amazed at the anger in her voice. She never spoke like that normally. And she could hear the echo of all of the things she wasn't saying as well: *Leave her alone, Accept her as she is, Let's not say anything else about it.*

Alissa was walking down the corridor towards them. Everyone welcomed her back and she responded with a genuine smile that lit up her whole face, especially her big, beautiful, hazel eyes. She was still quite thin, and her eyes looked strangely larger and more beautiful than ever. Zoe stood in the doorway to the classroom as she watched Alissa take all of her books out of her rucksack and put them away in her locker. She seemed quite calm and normal, but Zoe couldn't imagine what was going on in her mind, how she really felt. Sophie, Alissa's best friend – or at least the person she spent most time with at school – came down the corridor and went into the classroom. She headed straight for Alissa, hugging her and welcoming her back, as though they hadn't seen each other for ages, and she started telling her all of the latest news. 'Did you know that Madame Olenska's substitute's arriving today? Scary, eh?'

Leda came out of the toilets with her lips glistening suspiciously. She must have been sneakily trying on her new lip-gloss, thought Zoe. Her mum wouldn't let her wear make-up to school and it was against the rules anyway. Leda linked arms with Zoe and pulled her over to the window. 'What do you think? Does it suit me?'

'No,' Zoe blurted out, surprising herself for a second time, because she wasn't usually so direct. It was just that the golden orangey shade on her friend's lips made her look so much older. She seemed a world apart, so ridiculously grown-up. And the flash of belly-button peeping out between the bottom of her short T-shirt and the top of her baggy, low-slung trousers was just adding to the effect. 'Who are you?' she wanted to say to Leda. So she did just that.

'Zoe, you're such a weirdo sometimes,' Leda said affectionately. 'I know what you're saying, but I've just decided to get a bit more cool.'

'The only thing you're going to get is a cold,' Lucas whispered, coming up behind her.

'Oh look, another weirdo,' said Leda. She turned around, laughing, and rested her hands on Lucas's shoulders in a strangely intimate gesture, but then she pulled away as though she'd burned her fingers. She just stood there with her arms dangling at her sides, looking a little bewildered, as though she didn't quite know what she was doing.

Then the bell went, so they all had to go into the classroom and that was the end of it. Zoe and Leda shared a desk, of course – they had done since their first year at school. Zoe kept looking at her friend out of the corner of her eye with a strange, new awareness, a feeling that she'd somehow found out Leda's secret.

But there was no time to concentrate on those odd, confusing thoughts. The French teacher had come into the classroom and had started firing questions at the class, completely at random. You had to pay very close attention. It was like a shooting range and the next target could be you.

Zoe turned to look at the back row of the classroom, where Alissa was huddled in her seat, defensively. Perhaps she was worried that she might not be able to answer a question, that she'd missed something important. But when her turn came, she spoke confidently and calmly, and her answer was correct. The teacher gave a very slight nod and moved on to her next victim. Zoe sighed with relief. Welcome back, Alissa.

In the afternoon, they would finally find out what they'd all been dying to know. It was no surprise that everyone arrived early for their main dance lesson, the one usually taught by Madame Olenska. They hung around outside the room, in absolute silence, straining their ears to hear the voice on the other side of the door as it gave orders and made comments to the class before them. But with the music in the background, the shuffling of feet and the creaks of the floorboards, all that filtered through was an indistinct murmur. They couldn't even tell if it was a man or a woman, or even if it really *was* a voice that they could hear or just their imaginations working overtime.

'I saw a woman I didn't know in the secretary's office,'

Estelle whispered. 'She was really beautiful. She had black hair and a strange air of mystery about her. I think it must be her.'

'Shh,' said Laila, putting her finger to her lips. 'She's saying something.'

Laila was right. The music had stopped and it was definitely a woman speaking. She said just a few words, in a loud, strong voice that rang through the door. 'Okay. Thank you very much. I'll see you tomorrow.'

'She's got an accent. She sounds rather . . . exotic,' whispered Roberto.

Then the double doors opened wide and the Year Ten students filed out of the room. Zoe caught the eye of Lucy, who had helped her to lace up her shoes when she was small. They'd remained quite friendly since then. 'What's she like?' Zoe whispered to her.

'Strange,' said Lucy, smiling, and she walked off, with her head held high and her shoulders low. She looked as though she was floating a metre above the ground. Even though she was only a couple of years older than Zoe, Lucy had that graceful walk that all the older girls had without exception. Zoe sometimes watched herself in the mirror as she walked, but she never managed to look that elegant. Perhaps she was too young. Maybe it was a gift that a fairy gave to you on your fourteenth birthday, no sooner and no later.

It wasn't time to go in quite yet though. The windows

of the room were always opened wide for the required five minutes between classes for a change of air. Crowding round the door, they could see the mirrors that covered all of the walls, which meant they could see inside the room without actually going in. Everyone was very curious indeed.

There was a woman, just as they had thought, and she was unusually tall for a ballerina. Zoe shot a quick glance at Leda and could see that her long-limbed friend looked pleased. Leda was scared that she was going to grow too tall to be a ballerina. The teacher had very black, very short hair and that was another departure from the norm for ballerinas, who usually had a long mane of hair that they put up in a bun. She had huge eyes, which were very dark too, and she had eyebrows like seagulls' wings, which looked as though they had been drawn with a finger dipped into soot and which gave her an enquiring, alert expression, as though she were always on the lookout for something. Zoe could tell that she would never let anyone pull the wool over her eyes or catch her by surprise. She was wearing a black leotard with a low, scooped neckline and three-quarter-length sleeves. She was also wearing shimmering black tights, rather than the usual opaque ones. Zoe caught the flash of a short red wraparound skirt. She wasn't wearing ballet shoes but shoes with low heels and straps, like a flamenco dancer. And, suddenly,

Zoe realised that the new teacher was Spanish.

The teacher was picking out CDs for the lesson, but you could tell that she knew that lots of eyes were watching her. You could see it in the smile that was twitching at her lips – which were painted in a red that was as loud as her skirt. Was she going to be loud as well? Would she shout at them?

No, she didn't shout. She just closed the window, then gracefully turned to the door and said, 'Come in.' Her voice was low and warm and a little husky.

'I'm Alicia Gimenez and I'll be standing in for Madame Olenska while she's away,' she said. 'Please just call me Gimenez. Madame and I have agreed that while she's in Russia, we'll take the opportunity to work on strengthening your basic techniques. She expects to find a perfectly trained class upon her return. I know that you're very good, and I'm expecting a great deal from you. So, shall we get going?'

She looked at each of them in turn as they stood around the walls, in their usual positions, then pressed the button on the CD player. She had painted nails! Red nail varnish, of course.

Zoe suddenly thought of someone else who wasn't there – Maestro Fantin, the pianist. He always played the piano for their barre exercises, but he'd been ill and was taking a break to recover. The CD music was still good, but it never felt the same when Maestro Fantin wasn't there, and Zoe, who had learned to appreciate his company, was really missing him.

A slow piece of music filled the room. It was solemn and slightly hypnotic, with a motif that repeated over and over, accompanied by a rhythm of quiet drums in the background. It was so insistent that Zoe knew she wouldn't be able to get it out of her head for a while – that was good because it meant she'd be able to hum it for her dad later and he'd tell her what it was.

The music was great for the barre exercises, because the rhythm was so precise, but it was so soft and gentle at the same time that it buoyed up and supported her movements, making them feel fluid and relaxed. Zoe let herself be carried away by the *battements tendus*, which she usually found so boring. Foot forward, foot back, and one, and two – even that simple movement could hold a certain fascination. The really fascinating thing, though, was Gimenez . . . Was that really what they were going to call her? Why not Señora Gimenez? Or Señorita? Anyway, the really fascinating thing was that she was at the barre as well – Madame never did that! – performing the exercises with the calm precision of someone who had spent all of her life doing just that.

Well, I've spent almost all of my life doing nothing else too, thought Zoe as she tried to imitate her teacher's smooth, relaxed movements. *We're both doing the same thing.*

And that thought reassured her.

Then it was time for the exercises in the centre of the room. Gimenez (that still seemed odd, but maybe it was simpler just to use her surname – she didn't have the calm and laidback attitude of a Miss, but Mrs or Madame didn't sound right either, too dull and pompous) divided them into groups of four, mixing up boys and girls, as far as possible – though like all of the classes at the Academy, there were more girls than boys. She wanted them to perform a short sequence of jumps and pirouettes on the spot. She demonstrated once, twice, three times. Zoe couldn't take her eyes off her. The way she danced was so precise, but so natural. She moved from one position to the next so smoothly. Even the jumps, which could sometimes look unnatural (after all, you hardly ever jump in real life, do you?), seemed gentle and simple, the way she performed them. She seemed to look beyond the movement itself somehow. Perhaps that was how she pushed her limits. Isn't that what all dance really is, a way of pushing the body's limits?

Zoe laughed inwardly at all the complicated thoughts she was having. She emptied her mind of these thoughts, because now she had to pay attention and concentrate on the class as they all danced at the same time. She concentrated on Laila's perfect technique as she imitated the sequence, on the gentle strength that

Lucas brought to the dance and on Roberto's elevation, which was impeccable from a technical point of view, but was maybe a little more than the music required. Alissa did very well too – she was terribly thin, but so precise and so determined.

And then it was Zoe's turn and she hoped that she looked more relaxed than she felt. She tried to let the notes flow through her and to imitate that gentle way of dancing, with no rough edges, with no jolts or starts. Did she manage it? She wasn't sure. She certainly tried her hardest. It felt so strange to her, being so sharply focused on the inside, but so soft and gentle on the outside. Sharply soft. Softly sharp. Her English teacher would call that an oxymoron – that's when you put together two words that seem contradictory, which *are* contradictory, and the result is a strange clashing effect.

How very peculiar. Zoe had found a connection between English and dance. Making connections always seemed to be an obsession for teachers, taking a scientific subject and linking it to geography, to history, maybe even to maths – but, then again, what could you connect to maths? Leaning against the barre, as she watched her classmates repeating the same exercise, in their groups of four, Zoe had the feeling (a strange, wonderful, happy feeling) that dance wasn't just about dance, that it wasn't some difficult and magnificent thing that could only be done within the sheltered walls of the Academy, but that there was a secret, intense connection between dance and life. But then her thoughts became confused and once again she tried to turn her attention back to the exercises.

When the lesson was over and everyone ran to get changed and go home, Zoe looked at herself in the mirror in the dressing room. She saw the same old Zoe – neither tall nor short and still flat-chested. She felt as though the only part of her body that was growing was her mind – her head should be as fat and inflated as a balloon, considering the peculiar and complicated thoughts that lived inside it.

Leda laughed and gave her a nudge. 'Have you drifted off somewhere again? Are you telling the mirror all about your deepest desires? If you try asking it about Roberto, it'll give you the same answer every time . . .'

'Which is?' asked Zoe, rousing herself from her daze.

'Which is that he's in love with you! You should have seen the way he was looking at you when you were doing those pirouettes earlier. You were really good, by the way. You still haven't told me what you think of Miss Gimenez. I like her. She's so feminine, with her nails and her lipstick and everything . . . Maybe she'll let us wear make-up too. Just a bit.'

'I wouldn't get too excited,' said Zoe, shaking her head. 'But I like her too.'

'We'll see what she's like when it gets serious. Today she obviously just wanted to get to know us a bit. Soon we'll find out what she's after.'

'Why should she be after something?'

'Because she's a teacher, of course. They always want something. Attention. Obedience. Loyalty. That sort of thing.'

Her last words were a bit muffled, because Leda had bent over to tie up the endless laces of her new trainers, which were covered in a pretty flower design. They reminded Zoe that spring wasn't far away.

Zoe pulled on her old trainers – they were green and blue, but the colours had faded because they were so old and, to be honest, she was a bit fed up with them. As she did up the laces, she thought that all the really good teachers wanted was for you to find the right path for yourself. So did that mean that they wanted something? Yes, but not for themselves. They just wanted what was best for you.

'Um, Zoe . . .' Leda interrupted Zoe's train of thought. 'Those trainers . . .'

'Yeah, I know. You're absolutely right. I was just thinking the same thing. They're old and they've had it – or I've had it with them, at least. Will you come and look for a new pair with me on Saturday?'

Leda's face lit up. 'Of course I will. I've already got a couple of ideas . . .'

'Oh no. I'd better be ready for the fashion police,' said Zoe, smiling.

Leda sat down next to her and elbowed her in the side. 'You know, you really are funny sometimes.'

'Well, that makes two of us then, doesn't it?' laughed Zoe.

CHAPTER THREE

Lions and Swans

Gimenez really was a good teacher. When she demonstrated steps, she did it several times so that no one would be in any doubt about them, and sometimes she would stand beside one of the students or in a group and dance with them. That was always really helpful because her rhythm seemed to infect whoever she was standing next to. It was almost as if rhythm were contagious, but in a good way – anyone would be happy to catch it if it meant that you became a fabulous dancer, just like her.

The week flew by and, before Zoe knew it, it was

Friday evening and she was counting her savings to see how much money she had to spend on her new trainers. She realised that she could basically spend however much she wanted because, with her birthday and Christmas and unimaginative relatives, she'd managed to put aside quite a pile of money.

'Mum, I'm going shopping with Leda tomorrow,' she announced as she entered the kitchen. Her two sisters, Sara and Maria, were in their rooms. Her mum sat at the half-laid table, reading the paper and drinking a glass of white wine, which she always did when she was the one doing the cooking. When Zoe's dad cooked, her mum disappeared into the sitting room with a book until dinner was ready. Sometimes she was so engrossed in her reading that you had to call her three or four times. On this occasion, however, she looked up from the newspaper, blinked a bit and gave Zoe a suspicious look. 'I hope you're not going to go mad like you did the last time you went on a shopping spree,' she joked.

'No, I just need some new trainers. These ones are really awful,' said Zoe, holding up the mud-spattered shoes.

'You're right. They look like a couple of old rats,' said her mum. Zoe laughed.

'Shoes can cost a lot of money,' her mum continued. 'Have you decided how much you want to spend?'

'No. I thought I'd just wait and see what the shops had.'

'Bear in mind that you won't be able to wear them for very long – either your feet will grow or the shoes will go out of fashion. But I promise that when you've stopped growing, I'll buy you a pair of Manolo Blahniks.'

Manolo Blahnik shoes were a kind of legend in Zoe's family. Her mum had two pairs, with heels and without. One was a present from Zoe's dad and she bought the other pair as a birthday present for herself. Zoe preferred the pair without heels – they were black, very simple and flat, with ivy leaves sewn onto the straps, the kind of thing that a Greek goddess might wear. The ones with the high heels were more exciting. They were studded with beautiful little beads in a kind of tapestry of pink and green roses. When her mum wore them, she looked really glamorous, but Zoe preferred it when she looked like a mum.

'Can I go and try yours on? Just to see what they look like?' she asked.

'All right,' her mum agreed. 'But make sure you take those thick socks off first or you'll spoil the shape.'

Once out of her socks, her feet looked very white and a little bit damp, like a couple of slugs with too many feelers on the end. Instinctively, Zoe stretched out one foot in front of her, in mid-air, in a gesture that was so familiar that she didn't even need to think about it. There. Now it was beautiful – it didn't look like a slug any more, but like a ballerina's foot at work – strong and assured.

Her feet were transformed even more dramatically in the low sandals with the leaves on. She turned up her jeans so she could see her slim, elegant ankles.

'All a girl needs is a pair of shoes like that and she's dressed,' her mum said, appearing behind her in the doorway. Zoe looked at her mum's reflection in the mirror. She was only a little bit taller than Zoe now – Zoe had almost caught up with her. Her hair was pulled back and her face looked a bit tired and pinched, as it usually did at the end of a long day.

'You're right. I wouldn't have thought of it that way, but it's absolutely true,' said Zoe. Then, just for fun, she took off the black sandals and, with the utmost care, slipped the flowery ones out of their two matching bags and tried them on. It was a real effort lifting herself up on to the heels, and it felt really strange standing there in them, wobbling away, even with all her ballerina's sense of balance. She tried to take a few steps, felt herself swaying, then looked at herself in the mirror and laughed. 'I'll never get the hang of it.'

'Maybe you're more of a flatties type of person,' her mum suggested.

'They fit me, though. We're the same shoe size.'

'Does that mean you'll lend me your new trainers next time I go out with your dad?' her mum asked with a grin.

'We'll see,' said Zoe. 'Shoes are a very personal thing.'

But the next day, as she wandered through row after row of pumps and trainers, she found herself thinking that maybe that wasn't quite true. There were hundreds of them, all arranged on long shelves in the shop 'where absolutely everybody buys their shoes', as Leda had explained. And she seemed to be right, because there wasn't a design there that Zoe hadn't already seen a dozen times on the feet of people at school, in different colours and sizes perhaps but still the same old stuff.

'Which are the ones that are made by children?' she asked Leda, who was engrossed in her thoughts as she looked at a rack full of colourful belts.

'What?' Leda asked, dreamily.

'Which is the brand of shoes that exploits child labour in the Third World?' said Zoe, as though she were reciting a slogan. They'd read an article about it at school, but she didn't know much about labels, so she'd forgotten, even though she knew it was a well-known brand. Which one was it?

'No idea. Why are you so bothered? Anyway, it's not as if they're going to stick a label on them saying *Made by Six-year-old Kids*, is it?'

'I heard that they chain them up,' Zoe insisted. 'I'd rather buy from a nicer company.'

'Well, just ask the sales assistant then.'

They spent ages looking at all the different shoes. In

the end, tired and a bit fed up, Zoe dropped down on to a soft leather cube. As she sat there, her eyes fell upon a display that she hadn't noticed before. It included the same trainers as Leda's, but they were in loads of different styles – they came in all kinds of different colours, some with patterns printed on them, others with flowers and hearts and shapes.

'I like those ones,' she said to Leda, pointing at a pair in a green and brown camouflage design.

'Good choice. They're a classic. And they're not too expensive either,' Leda remarked.

Finally, after trying several pairs on, Zoe was ready to buy some. They went over to pay, but the queue was really long. It was as if everyone in town had suddenly decided that they absolutely had to get something new to wear that Saturday afternoon. They were nearly at the front of the queue when Zoe heard a sudden gasp from behind her. She looked at Leda and saw that her face was really pale. She was huddling up behind Zoe, trying to make herself as small as possible. 'Hide me, Zoe.'

Zoe did as she was told, and looked around to see if she could spot the reason for Leda's sudden attack of weirdness. A-ha. There was the reason. Leo and Haydée had just come into the shop, and had stopped in front of a display of jackets. He had his arm around her shoulders and she had her arm around his waist.

'It must be your turn soon. Or let's just go? Please?'

Leda begged, her voice slightly muffled against Zoe's back. Zoe did everything she could so that they'd be finished quickly – she made sure she had exactly the right money. At last, it was her turn and quickly – scan, bag, receipt – they were done. Fortunately, there was another exit on the other side of the shop and the rows of clothes and shoes provided quite a few handy hiding places on the way.

Leda and Zoe managed to leave without being spotted. Outside, the bright afternoon sun was shining. The afternoons had been really bright for a few days now. Even though she was already familiar with them, the beauty of the seasons could always surprise Zoe. Leda pushed Zoe forwards anxiously, moving away from the shop in a frantic rush. They hurried all the way down the long and crowded street. Then they found themselves in front of Zoe's favourite cake shop and decided to pop in. As the shoes hadn't cost too much, Zoe could treat them to something sweet and sticky, which seemed like just the right thing to do.

Five minutes later, they were sitting in front of a selection of tiny little cakes, but Leda had the empty gaze of someone who couldn't see beyond the end of her own nose. It was as though she'd been swallowed up by the fog of her own misery. She wasn't speaking or eating or drinking – Zoe was glad she wasn't crying. She wanted to be sympathetic but couldn't help but be distracted by the plate in front of them. That little cake with pink icing was calling out to her, tempting her. *Eat me.* Maybe it was like the cake in *Alice's Adventures in Wonderland* and one bite would turn you into a giant. Or the size of a tiny little ant. If that happened, who would pay the bill when she was hiding away under the table, trying not to get trampled on? Leda had left her money at home to avoid any temptation.

As the icing gave way beneath Zoe's teeth and the cream spread deliciously over her tongue, Leda finally spoke.

'He told me he wanted us to be special friends,' she said. 'He told me I was special. I thought he was going to ask *me* out.'

Leda hadn't ever told her that Leo had said that, and it upset her to see Leda so miserable. The fact that Leda was talking about Leo in the past tense was a slight sign of hope, though – she seemed to know that he was never going to ask her out.

Zoe had never liked Leo. He was too snobby, too much of a poser, always so showy and perfect. He and Haydée had arrived together at the beginning of the school year, the two new students. Zoe didn't think Haydée was very nice either. She hadn't made friends with anyone else, so it was natural that she and Leo had become close. Maybe they were a good match for each other, but that was no reason for him to string Leda along.

Leda was always saying that Leo was such a noble name. She'd kept going on about it since he'd arrived at the school. Well, there was certainly nothing noble about him. He was a schemer and a cheat. Leo meant 'lion', after all, and Zoe told Leda that he also had a big head like a lion.

Leda snapped at her. 'What are you talking about? He's really handsome. Take a good look at your perfect Roberto before you start criticising.'

Zoe didn't feel angry, not even the slightest bit. She knew Leda was just upset, and the best thing was to take her comments with good grace and to focus on the other cakes that were calling out to her. *Eat me. Eat me.* Should she eat in such a crisis? Absolutely. It was her duty.

Leda peered into her teacup as though wondering if there were any tea leaves in the bottom of it that she could read. Or maybe she was dreaming that her tea would turn into a really strong poison that she could slip to the treacherous Leo. A lethal dose. A swift death, perhaps a very painful one. Haydée would be allowed to live, all on her own, an outcast. Leo was the guilty one, wasn't he?

'Look, why don't you have one of those cakes with the chocolate on?' Zoe suggested after a while. 'They're your favourite.'

'Might as well,' said Leda. 'Doesn't matter if I get fat now.'

And within a few minutes, all of the chocolate cakes

had disappeared. All of the tea had gone as well. It had transformed from a terrible poison into a healing potion. Zoe's gran always said that a cup of tea solved everything. Of course, Zoe knew that wasn't really true – it was one of those exaggerations that you always find in proverbs and expressions. Wise words, but false ones,which were just designed to make you feel better. But the tea really was good, and so were the cakes.

Zoe went to the counter and paid the bill. With their stomachs full, their mouths still sweet with the taste of the cakes, the colours of the late afternoon in their eyes, and a bag with a pair of new shoes dangling from Zoe's wrist, the journey home was a pleasure. Zoe and Leda held hands, as if they were little girls at playgroup. Leda hadn't shed one single tear for that slimeball Leo. That was a good sign. Zoe reckoned that it was best to leave things as they were and say no more about it. Leo might be like a lion, but Leda's name meant 'swan'. Deep down, Zoe knew that Leda would soon be ready to fly again.

CHAPTER FOUR

A
Phone Call

'Hello there. It's Zoe.'

'Oh, Zoe! Sweetheart. It's so nice to hear from you,' said Alice's mum. 'How are you?'

'I'm fine, thanks. How are things with you?'

'Well, the boys aren't great. They both keep catching the latest bug that's going around. Alice seems to be a bit more robust though. I'll go and fetch her for you.'

Zoe waited a moment and listened to the footsteps moving away from the phone and then different footsteps running towards it. Then there was Alice's voice, a little out of breath, on the other end of the line.

Being long-distance friends is difficult, thought Zoe, but not impossible. You can keep in touch by text and there's always the telephone and email for longer conversations. Text messages might seem easiest, but they're too short to be any good really. If you sent five, six or even ten, *that* might be enough to say what you wanted. But they're so tiny – even with all the abbreviations and smilies, you can't always manage to include everything that you feel like saying.

So, every now and then, Zoe and Alice, the friend she met last summer on holiday in the mountains, had a nice, quiet chat on the phone. Zoe had made herself comfortable. She was sitting on the floor, leaning against the wall, with the soles of her feet pressed together and her legs in a kind of diamond shape.

'Hi, Zoe. What's up?'

Zoe laughed. 'So if I phone you something has to be up, does it?'

'Well, I hope you're not going to start telling me all about your grades at school instead, because I'll tell you now, I'd prefer not to talk about anything school-related. It's a bit of a touchy subject at the moment. I got seventeen out of twenty in our maths test. Rubbish, eh?'

'Well, actually . . .'

Zoe was good at maths and so was Alice. Seventeen out of twenty wasn't a bad score, but if someone usually got nineteen or twenty out of twenty, it was a different matter.

'It's all right, you can calm down,' said Zoe. 'I didn't phone to talk about school.'

'A-ha. I see. So you want to talk about Roberto then.'

'Hmm . . . you're just too clever by half.'

'I know you, Zoe, and I know exactly what's going on in your life. I'm like a fortune-teller. Madame Alice sees all, knows all. It's quite simple, really. So, how *are* things with Roberto?'

'Everything's fine. Great, actually. He's so sweet and kind and affectionate. I like him because he's a friend *and* more than a friend. I like spending time with him. It feels really natural and comfortable. I don't have to pretend to be something I'm not, the way you see some girls doing. You know, always talking at the top of their voices to attract attention and wearing so much make-up that they look like clowns; they're really just playing at being grown-up.'

'You're so lucky. I really like Guy, but I don't know how to make him notice I exist.'

'Guy? Who's that then?'

'Oh, he's in my brother Ed's class at school. They haven't always been friends, but I'd seen him around. Now he's started to come over to our place and they do their homework together. Sometimes he sleeps over at the weekend . . .'

'Well, at least he's within easy reach . . .'

'Not exactly. You know what boys are like. They shut

themselves away and play on the games console and don't surface again until the evening.'

'Yes, but they do come out to eat, don't they?'

'That's true. I give him my best adoring look over dinner. Then, luckily, Mum and Dad won't let them play after dinner, so we usually watch a film together.'

'So you give him your best adoring look over the popcorn instead, right?'

'Right. And over the ice cream. And the crisps. And the M&Ms. I eat so much food when I'm thinking about him. It makes me hungry. It makes me starving!'

'If you carry on like that, you're going to turn into a whale.'

'I know. Fat and unhappy. Ha ha ha.'

'Do you know what, Alice? For someone who's supposed to be lovesick, you sound pretty cheerful.'

'That's because I *am* cheerful. Isn't it wonderful, being in love in the springtime?'

'So, do you think it's better to be fat and happy or thin and unhappy?' Zoe giggled.

'Fat and happy, that's for sure,' Alice laughed.

'And weird. You're weird too. Don't forget about that!'

'Absolutely. That's me! Fat and happy and weird.'

'Yep, you're so weird that, before long, people will be paying to come and stare at you.'

And that's how the phone call went on and eventually finished: on a silly, cheerful note that was perfectly in tune with the spirit of the season that had just begun. Zoe was happy that her friend had fallen for someone – so happy that she actually forgot to tell her exactly why she'd phoned, which was that Roberto had given her a silver ring. Just like that, for no reason, because 'there doesn't always have to be a reason for a present, does there?' Zoe thought that was the best reason of all. The ring was silver, a delicate filigree knot, and it was slightly too big for her, so she had to wear it on her thumb. She kept fiddling with it, constantly turning it around in her fingers, partly because it was new and made her hand feel strange, and partly because she liked touching it and feeling that it was there. She'd decided that when she was fed up with wearing it on her thumb, she'd hang it around her neck. She had a silk ribbon with two strands in different shades of pink and she'd already tried it out. It looked really good.

But did it mean something if someone gave you a ring? When she showed the ring to her sister, Sara opened her big blue eyes really wide, and just said, 'Wow!' She asked Zoe if she could try it on and then she held up her hand and studied the ring, the way women do in those old American movies, when they're showing off their engagement rings. Zoe felt a bit like laughing, but she managed to hold it in.

'So, he's serious about you,' Sara commented.

'Don't be daft,' said Zoe, blushing.

'Aw, my little sister's growing up,' said Sara. It sounded to Zoe as though Sara was just the tiniest bit jealous. 'When did he give it to you?'

Fortunately, a phone call from one of Sara's friends interrupted their conversation. Sara disappeared into her room to gossip and swap notes about homework, and so Zoe didn't have to answer her question. That was a relief because she would have had to say that she didn't want to tell Sara, and that would have been rude – Sara would have been offended and maybe they'd have ended up having an argument. But there are some things that are better if you keep them to yourself and don't share them with anyone. Tiny, secret moments that you can revisit when you're alone because they make you feel good inside.

She and Roberto had been in the park one Saturday afternoon. It was the classic romantic spot, but they'd only gone that way because it was the quickest route to the cinema, where some other friends were meeting them. There was one free bench. All of the others were occupied by couples who were obviously much older than them – proper couples, grown-ups who were busy kissing or whispering to each other. Two of them were arguing, though – they were a long way off, but you could tell from the jerky way they were moving their heads and hands that they were saying things that were designed to hurt. Roberto suddenly stopped and pulled Zoe over to the empty bench. Then he dug around in his jeans pocket and took out the shiny ring and presented it to her, between his thumb and forefinger. 'It's for you,' he said and placed it in her open hand.

Zoe took the ring but didn't put it on immediately. Instead she closed her hand round it and felt how warm the ring was from the heat of Roberto's body.

'Thank you,' she said. And she slipped it into her pocket. All the ring had done was move from one pocket to another. No one had said any big and meaningful words. *Just as well*, thought Zoe. *We're too young for that kind of thing*.

They looked into each other's eyes for a moment, right up close. *When you usually see an eye from so close, it looks a bit scary*, thought Zoe. She'd often thought that when she was looking at her own eyes in the mirror – the white part, the iris with all those colours arranged in little lines, the shifting black pupil and the lashes, like a row of little spikes. But Roberto's eyes, even up close, were beautiful and they didn't scare Zoe at all. A quick kiss – just a brush of the lips – and Zoe pulled Roberto to his feet. They had to run then because they were late meeting the others. Afterwards, it felt almost as though they hadn't met up with anyone at all, because they all went straight into the cinema and the film started five minutes later. In the darkness, Zoe found that she wasn't focusing on the film at all, but playing with the ring inside her pocket.

CHAPTER FIVE

Movit
Are Here!

Lucas was late to class the next morning and he just couldn't sit still at his desk. He kept fidgeting around in his seat and he dropped three books and his pencil case, creating an explosion of pens and rubbers and pencils all over the classroom. Zoe and Leda looked at each other but didn't say anything: their French teacher was already in a bad mood and had threatened to give detention to anyone who caused any trouble. But the look on Leda's face said, 'What's up with Lucas?'

'No idea,' Zoe's expression replied.

They had to wait until breaktime to find out. Lucas

was bursting to tell them – he didn't just run into the corridor, he threw himself into the air with one of those long jumps that only he could do and, as he landed, he yelled out, 'Have you seen the poster outside the theatre? Movit are coming!'

Movit were Lucas's favourite dance company. They performed a kind of contemporary dance that was elastic, athletic and entertaining, full of colour and extravaganza and acrobatics, and Lucas was absolutely mad about them. Whenever they came to town he went to see their shows at least twice. They'd let him down last year, because they didn't visit the Academy Theatre on their tour, and he had been very upset. He still managed to see them though when he was on holiday in America, and he'd been absolutely over the moon, even though it was a show he'd already seen. This time, however, they were putting on a new show.

'It's called *Angels*,' he sighed. '*Angels*. Isn't that wonderful?'

'You should at least wait to see it before deciding that,' said Leo, trying to dampen his enthusiasm.

'But I know that they're going to be fantastic and the show's going to be great,' said Lucas with a certainty that was so full of adoration it verged on disturbing.

'Have you got tickets yet? I have,' boasted Leo with a smirk. 'My dad knows someone through work who got him half-price tickets.'

He was so unpleasant. Leda gave him a withering look. Lucas didn't pay any attention though, because he was so wrapped up in his own world. He was mumbling a list of strange words: *Magnum Opus, Stars Moon Sun, Basketball, Obsession* . . .

'What's he going on about now?' sneered Leo.

'They're the names of the other shows that Movit have done,' explained Zoe with a patience she didn't know she had. She could have added 'idiot' at the end, but she managed to stop herself. Leda didn't though.

'So you're boasting about having tickets but you don't even know the names of their shows?' Leda said.

Leo went red, his cheeks flushing brightly, which didn't suit him at all.

'Whatever. I'll just have a look at the programme,' he said defensively, but no one was listening to him now.

'Why don't we all go together?' asked Leda, launching into one of her big plans to organise everyone. 'We could go for a Sunday matinee, so it'll be over early and we can do something else with the rest of the afternoon. I'll sort out the tickets. Who wants to come?'

And as she counted the number of people who wanted to go, she deliberately turned her back on Leo, who was standing right beside her, leaving him out. He turned on his heels and walked away.

Zoe wanted to feel at least a little sorry for him, but she couldn't. Instead she listened to Lucas's dreamy account of the last Movit show he'd seen, with dancers who were as round and prickly as cactus plants in the desert, or who unfurled like umbrellas, or floated like strange, melancholy aquatic plants.

That evening, at home, she went online to find out about this *Angels* show. The Academy Theatre website had an article about it, with lots of absolutely wonderful photographs. The site said that the show was a series of short dances, inspired by famous paintings featuring angels of different kinds: cherubs, warrior angels, avenging angels, as well as the princes of heaven who had fallen into hell, where they danced among the flames. It looked absolutely fascinating. But the show wasn't for another six weeks, so there'd be plenty of time to talk about it and to find out more.

But it actually turned out that she didn't have to wait that long. The next day Lucas dashed down the entire length of the corridor and stopped with perfect precision right in front of Leda, Roberto and Zoe, then announced breathlessly, 'They're already here! They're rehearsing *here!*'

There was no need to ask who he was talking about. Movit were the only thing on his mind.

'That's a bit strange, isn't it?' asked Leda, and she was right. Dance companies usually arrived just a week before the performance, sometimes even less – allowing just enough time to check out the theatre and have a few rehearsals before the first show.

'Yeah. They were supposed to be putting the show together at home in America, but the theatre there brought forward its renovation work, so they couldn't use the rehearsal rooms. So, instead of moving to a nearby town, they asked if they could come here early and they've moved everything to the Academy Theatre. I think I'm going to go insane! Movit at the Academy!'

'So have you thought about how you're going to get close to them?' Leda smiled.

'Of course. I'm going to ambush them,' Lucas said with a big grin.

'But they won't let you anywhere near the theatre. It's a world premiere,' said Zoe gently. She didn't want to seem pessimistic, but she didn't want Lucas to be disappointed either.

'I'll find a way. You'll see,' Lucas assured her. And, judging by the glint in his eye, he obviously had a plan.

Two days later, Zoe was leaving school when she bumped into Lucas wearing black trousers, a white shirt and a deep-red bow tie, with a white apron tied around his waist and a clinking tray of glasses held at shoulder height. She wasn't at all surprised.

'Is this your big plan?' she whispered to him.

'Shh, don't give me away,' he whispered back to her, as he took short, precise steps towards the stage door.

Zoe gave in to her curiosity and followed him. She watched as he cautiously pushed open the door and the glasses on the tray clattered and banged together. Once he was through the door, she could see him walking on with determination, even though he was just a vague shape through the frosted glass. One of the new security guards would have to be on duty for Lucas to get through, because everyone else in the theatre knew him. But Zoe waited for ten minutes and didn't hear any shouting or uproar or the crash of broken glass. It was unbelievable. He'd done it! He'd have a story to tell her tomorrow.

Lucas didn't even wait until the next day to tell Zoe, but phoned her that evening. He told her excitedly that he'd managed to sneak into the dressing rooms by saying that he was bringing a delivery from the bar. One of the Movit dancers actually became quite indignant, saying that child labour should be prohibited ('Isn't it illegal for such young people to work in your country?'), and Lucas calmed him down by saying that it was his dad's bar and that he just helped him out for an hour or two after school, but only when he was really needed and after he'd finished his homework.

He'd come out with a tray full of empty cups and glasses and a handful of autographs, and he was wild with excitement. He'd never managed to get their autographs before, even though he always went round to the stage door to say hello after the show – it was so chaotic and full of people saying hi and smiling and complimenting the dancers that a boy like Lucas became practically invisible.

'There's one guy who's really nice. He's called Lucky and he's black like me,' he told her. 'His costume was hanging up in the dressing room. It was an angel costume, of course, but it was made out of black rubber that looked like liquorice. He must be one of the fallen angels. The costume's got wings, but they're made out of scales, not feathers, like they're reptile wings or something. It made you want to touch them, because they're not how you'd imagine a pair of wings. They've got some kind of coating on them so that the scales glisten and look like dragons' wings.'

'You're already thinking about your next step, aren't you?' asked Zoe. Lucas's next move was bound to involve sneaking into the rehearsals somehow.

'Of course I am,' he said, smiling.

'Are you going to pretend to be the boy from the bar again?'

'I don't think so. I checked the guards' work schedule. The usual guys are on for the next five days. They'd catch me straightaway and I just can't take the risk. I'll come up with another idea. See you tomorrow!'

Zoe had no doubt that Lucas would find a way. For him, seeing Movit, and seeing them as many times as he could, was the most important thing ever.

At school the next day, a ball of paper rolled across the floor and came to a stop beneath Zoe's desk. She spotted the movement out of the corner of her eye, dropped a biro on the floor and bent over to pick it up, along with the piece of paper.

BIG NEWS!!! the note said, written in capitals as though someone was shouting it out loud. It was followed by: *TELL YOU AT BREAKTIME.*

When the bell went, Lucas didn't even wait to leave the classroom. He dashed over to Zoe and Leda's desk, leaned his hands on it and did an elegant leap with a scissor kick. Then he said, 'This is fantastic! You're not going to believe this – *I* can't believe it! They need a boy dancer! They need me!'

Leda and Zoe waited for him to continue, which didn't happen for a while, because Lucas had taken his hands off their desk and was executing a series of pirouettes in mid-air to show just how happy he was. Once he had landed, he started talking again. 'There's a part for a little angel. They told us this morning in gym. Movit are going to choose from the boys who are between twelve and fourteen. It's perfect, isn't it?'

Leda cast a glance at Zoe, hesitated, then finally blurted out, 'Yes, it's perfect. But if there's just one part, how are you so certain it's going to be you?'

'That's easy. Because I really want it,' Lucas answered.

And with another series of pirouettes he disappeared out of the classroom. You could imagine him pirouetting down the entire length of the corridor, in a magnificent solo of pure joy.

'Let's keep our fingers crossed,' Zoe said to Leda. 'It'll be terrible if he doesn't get it.'

The auditions were a few days later, in the early evening. In total, fifteen boys were taking part. Leda and Zoe hung around on the steps outside the school and ate three chocolate biscuits each while they waited. When they saw Lucas coming, they only had to look at the misery on his face to see how it had gone.

'They picked Roberto,' he said. 'They picked Roberto.' Then he turned and walked away.

Leda and Zoe didn't follow him. They looked at each other, miserably. Then they got up and left, feeling a weight on them that was partly the biscuits in their stomachs, and partly something else.

When she was at home that evening, Zoe received a text message from Roberto. *I'm sorry* it said. *I'm really sorry. :(*

He obviously didn't know what to say and Zoe didn't phone him so he didn't have to talk about it. She just sent him a message that was simple and true: *Not your fault. I'm happy for you.*

It was really strange that they'd picked Roberto. He was very good, but his style of dance was so much more technical, more classical than Lucas's. Lucas was so fluid in his movements, so natural, that he seemed to be a born member of Movit. But maybe, Zoe thought, that was exactly what they wanted: the purity of a young angel. The way Lucas danced was more unsettling. When he moved, you couldn't take your eyes off him, even if he was just walking. He attracted you like a magnet, while Roberto was calm and serene. Yes, definitely more angelic.

For the first time, Zoe felt torn between her feelings for two people that she was fond of, but in different ways. She was happy for Roberto, but her happiness was clouded because she felt so sorry for Lucas. Did that mean she cared more about Roberto or Lucas? Lucas had been her friend for ever and ever. Roberto had arrived on the scene later, but their relationship was different. So who did she owe her loyalty to? Both of them, of course. But she didn't like feeling so divided, with her heart split in two by a crack that was thin but deep.

Two days passed. Lucas kept himself to himself, isolated, curled up as tightly as a hedgehog. It was so unusual for him to behave that way that everyone noticed. Everyone knew why, of course.

'They took the best dancer,' hissed Leo.

Leda, who was completely over her crush on Leo

now, blew her top. 'What would you know about it, new boy?' It was a quick and effective way of excluding him. Leo was always going to be the new boy, even in five years' time, because he was such an outsider, so different from the rest of them who had been together for such a long time already.

Laila, who was usually so spiteful, said nothing, which was odd, but it was probably because it wasn't something that involved her. Alissa sighed as she looked at Lucas. He was staring out of the window as if an entirely new landscape had suddenly appeared out there. 'It's so unfair,' she said.

As they left school that afternoon, Roberto came over to Zoe with a big grin on his face. 'Have you heard the news?' he said. 'We had a dress rehearsal today and I'm allergic to the rubber. I put on the angel's wings and helmet and just started itching and scratching. Look,' he said, and he pulled down his jumper and showed Zoe the skin on his neck, which still looked really raw, and the long scratches that he'd made with his own nails. 'It means I can't dance the part, so they've had to choose someone else instead. Their next choice was Lucas. He's in the rehearsals right now. He's not allergic to the rubber – in fact, he loves the costume!'

'But why are you so happy?' Zoe asked him, a little taken aback.

'Because it wasn't so important to me. I mean, it

would have been great, but it's not the thing that I want most in the world, like it is for Lucas. So it's good that it's worked out this way.'

Zoe smiled and took his hand. So, everything had worked out fine in the end. Wasn't that wonderful? The crack in her heart sealed up immediately and she felt as though a weight had been lifted from her.

CHAPTER SIX

Good Books
and Bad Books

'There was this man who was a bit strange and he lived in this old garage that was falling to pieces and he was all covered in bits and pieces of things that he'd eaten, and he smelled like an old man and he seemed just like an old man, but then the boy realised that he was actually an angel, because he had these two wings on his back, but the wings were just as ugly as the rest of him and they were kind of gross as well. Then the boy took him some Chinese food to eat because the man kept on repeating these numbers and the boy realised that they were the numbers on a Chinese takeaway menu, and this old angel guy really loved Chinese food. Do you like Chinese food? At the restaurant near my house, number 48 is Cantonese rice. I know that because I'm always the one who phones up to place the order, but I can't remember what the numbers in the book are. That doesn't really matter, though, does it?'

It was absolutely ridiculous. The more Zoe listened, the more ridiculous the whole thing seemed. Their English supply teacher had asked Paula to tell her about a book that they were supposed to read. Their usual teacher made them choose books from a list of titles that she suggested at the beginning of the year and they had to read them at home or whenever there was spare time at school – for instance when they'd finished their work early or at the end of a lesson. She'd never dream of asking you to talk about a book in class though, even if that meant that some people never read the books; Zoe just figured it was their loss.

The supply teacher was getting a bit impatient with Paula's ramblings, but she was the one who had asked, so it served her right if she had to listen to Paula's insane speech.

There seemed to be angels all over the place lately. Zoe turned round to look at Lucas, who was doodling in the margins of his exercise book. Even from a distance you could tell that he was drawing wings – little fluffy wings for cherubs, huge feathered wings for angels and archangels. Zoe wondered what the Movit wings were like that he'd have to wear. White or black? He'd look better in white wings, she thought.

Leda was wearing a new T-shirt. It was white with pink trim and sleeves and had a chubby little angel shooting an arrow on the front, a Cupid with big round eyes like a fawn. Estelle's new earrings had two little angels with blue wings on them. She took them off for dance lessons, but always put them straight back on as soon as they were back in the changing room.

Phew, Paula had finished. The supply teacher just nodded and didn't make any comment about what she'd said. That's what supply teachers were all about — torturing you for no good reason. Zoe cheered with everyone else when a teacher was away, but she always found that, before too long, she wished they'd come back.

'It's a good book, *Skellig*,' Zoe said to Paula at breaktime as they all went outside. 'I like David Almond's other books as well. Have you read them? There's just one that's a bit tricky. It's called *Counting Stars*, which is a beautiful title, but they're stories about him and I think that they're maybe better for grown-ups.'

'I'm not really into reading,' Leda said. 'Apart from romantic novels. I'm reading one now about a girl who ends up as the girlfriend of the son of the president of the United States.'

'Wouldn't it be more interesting if she became the president herself?' said Paula.

'My mum's just bought me a book with a big picture of a wing on the cover. You know, because of the Movit show,' Lucas interrupted. He clearly had only one thing on his mind and absolutely everything centred upon that. 'It's called *The Icarus Girl* and the author wrote it when she was only eighteen. She's some kind of genius. It must be difficult to write a book when you're that young, mustn't it? Anyway, my mum said it would be lucky for me.'

'You reckon it's going to bring you luck? You know what happened to Icarus, don't you?' Jamie laughed. '*Wheee . . .*' He spread his arms and mimed plummeting to the ground.

'Whatever,' Lucas replied. 'It's the thought that counts. Anyway, it's a really beautiful cover.'

'Is that right? You always choose a book for the cover, do you?' asked Stephanie.

'Well, partly, yes,' said Lucas, almost sounding offended. 'What's so bad about that? If a book's got a nice cover, you want to open it up and have a look.'

'Yes, but the story might be really dull,' said Paula. 'I always read the blurb on the back and the beginning of the book too, at least half of the first page. I can tell straightaway if it's going to be interesting. But I might not actually like it as such. There are some things that can be interesting without you liking them. For example, *Skellig* is a really sad book, and I don't really like books that make you cry and feel miserable. You know, those ones where you want the story to change when it gets too gloomy? I prefer books about feelings. But then sadness is a feeling too, I suppose . . .' She trailed off, as though she'd lost the thread of what she was saying.

'Yes, but the ending's good,' said Zoe.

'You think so? It finishes well for the baby girl, but he . . .'

Francine put her hands over her ears. 'Stop it. Stop it. I don't want to hear how it ends! You've got me interested and I want to read it. Please don't tell me what happens.'

Zoe and Paula laughed. Then Paula said, 'How come you boys never read anything?'

'That's not true,' protested Jamie. 'I always read my PlayStation magazines.'

'Hmm, you must find some wonderful stories in those,' Stephanie laughed.

'There aren't any stories in them, stupid. It's all about tips for finishing levels, and reviews of different games,' said Matthew, very seriously. 'And there's a CD with demos so that you can try out games that have just come out and if you like them you can go and buy them, or decide not to bother. I tried out the latest *Grand Theft Auto* and I really loved it, but my mum said that it was too violent, so she wouldn't let me buy it.'

'Wow, Matthew, I've never heard you say so much in one go,' said Sophie, teasing him. Matthew's face went bright red, but he still ended up laughing.

When breaktime was over, there was one more lesson with the supply teacher from hell, but as she had no idea what to do with the class, she just let them do homework or study their books for the next day. Zoe was a bit fed up, because she'd already done everything and she didn't even have a book with her. She hadn't decided yet whether she liked the one she was reading at the moment, because it wasn't one single story, but lots of different episodes – sort of like short stories. They were a bit strange, about two kids who lived in a city and did all the normal stuff that kids do – going out with friends, buying things, listening to music – and their lives kept on touching each other, but they never actually crossed paths. Zoe thought that something was going to happen at any moment to bring them together, but nothing like that had happened yet, so she just kept on wondering where the author was going with the story and whether he might just be teasing her.

As everything seemed to be about angels right now, Zoe thought about how there were some books that actually seemed to have wings. They suddenly took flight on page two, sometimes even on the very first page, and carried you away and you couldn't manage to tear yourself away right until the end. You kept on doing all the usual things, of course, but you spent every free moment inside the book and when it was finished you felt a bit sad, because you wanted it to go on and on for ever and ever, but at the same time you wanted to find out how it was going to end. There were other books too that were so heavy going – the kind of books that had no spark at all and the words felt like snails crawling over the page and you felt like a snail yourself as you were reading them, so slowly that eventually you stopped moving. You couldn't manage even another comma, so you gave up and closed the book and forgot the story and it was much better that way. As she was thinking all of these things, Zoe was doing little doodles on half a sheet of squared paper that she'd torn out of her notebook. She filled the squares with little lines and circles and tiny pictures, using a purple felt-pen with a very fine tip. She was working away patiently at something that was completely pointless, and she knew it, but it was a way to kill time.

'I'm so glad our real teacher's coming back on Monday. I can't stand the thought of any more supply teachers,' Leda grumbled as they were stretching their legs before the last lesson.

'But Gimenez is great,' Alissa pointed out. 'I like the way she teaches. I mean, Madame's Madame, but I think a bit of a holiday at home will be doing her some good.'

'How do you mean?' Zoe asked her, curiously. Since she'd come back, Alissa seemed a lot better. She was interested and alert and she did everything with precision and enthusiasm. She'd moved away a bit from Sophie, who had always been her best friend, and sometimes she spent time with Zoe and Leda. She'd also changed the way she dressed. She'd given up her usual flashy colours and had started wearing pastel shades that definitely suited her better.

'Well, over the years, Madame Olenska has developed these really definite ideas about what we're all like, and it's almost as if we're stuck with them now,' she said, warming to her subject. 'You know, as far as she's concerned, you're the same Zoe as when you were six years old, with all the same good points and bad points. But people can change. Take me, for example. I don't want her to look at me with those scary eyes of hers and think that I'm just the same old Alissa. I really have changed.'

She said it with the voice of someone who was trying to convince herself, nodding her head as if she was saying yes all the while. But it really was true. It was as though she'd finally understood what her problem was, and once she'd managed to confront it, she'd solved the problem. Zoe admired her for that. Some of the other girls, though, were a bit suspicious. They were wary around her, as if she were ill and contagious. That certainly wasn't going to help her to feel better. But Alissa was brave and was getting better and eating more now.

Gimenez's lesson that afternoon was particularly brilliant. After an unusually short session on the barre, she called them into the centre of the room, two by two, to perform one of those steps where the dancers cross arms and hold hands, only she mixed up the class a bit and created five couples of boys and girls. For the first time, Zoe found herself dancing with Roberto. It was strange, considering that they spent practically the whole of every school day together, that it had never happened before. If a teacher ever suggested forming mixed couples, Zoe instinctively went over to Lucas if he hadn't already made his way to her. That was because they'd known each other for so many years, and dancing with a friend wasn't the same as dancing with a, with a . . . whatever Roberto was. A boyfriend? Was that too serious? So what was he then?

Now wasn't the time to think about it. She was used to having complete control over her body, so she took hold of Roberto's hands, which were dry and warm, and repeated the steps that Gimenez showed them, concentrating on the sequence, on pointing her toes, on keeping her shoulders low, on the delicate movements of her head. She was imagining and hoping that Roberto was doing the same, because when you're dancing in a couple it's not enough for one person to be good, the two of you have to be good together and in the same way, with the same casual confidence. You can't watch yourselves in the mirror. You just have to have faith in yourselves and in the way your bodies respond to the orders that your minds send out. One, two, this way. Three, four, that way. And one, two, again. And three, four, there. And again, again, again, again . . .

'Good,' said Gimenez. 'Very good. Is the next couple ready? Come along then!'

Once she had returned to her rest position with her arms leaning on the barre, Zoe felt like an angel, with wings on her heels and on her back. Roberto had gone back to the boys' side of the room. Zoe looked over and caught his eye. She saw his little smile that was meant just for her. Oh, those angels. They really were everywhere!

CHAPTER SEVEN

Old Friends

One morning before lessons, Zoe walked past two of the dance teachers in the corridor, which was the breeding ground for vicious gossip. The teachers taught the older classes and Zoe hoped she'd never, ever have them when she was older. One was saying to the other, 'He's back again, that Fantin man. He's such a pain. If it's not one thing with him, it's another. First he's ill, then he takes off on holiday. When someone's that age, they really should just stay at home.'

The other replied, 'You know that he actually should have retired a while ago, don't you? But Olenska still lets him come in. She's too soft-hearted to be headmistress.'

And that was all she heard. They'd walked past and turned the corner. Zoe was amazed to hear Madame Olenska described as soft-hearted – she usually seemed the exact opposite – but she was happy to hear that Madame was the reason Maestro Fantin was still working at the Academy. Then she thought about how mean the first teacher had been. She was furious by the time she'd climbed the stairs to the second floor, where she knew that Maestro Fantin was going to be accompanying the first lesson for the little ones. It was ten minutes before class, just enough time for a quick hello.

Well before she reached the room, a cloud of music floated towards her, enveloping her from head to toe. It was intense music, a little gloomy, with lots of flourishes and the suggestion of an approaching storm. It couldn't have been more different from the simple melodies with their strong rhythms that Maestro Fantin usually played to accompany the rigid discipline of their barre exercises. She stopped at the door and didn't push it open until the echoes of the final chord had finally died away. She took a step inside the door. 'May I come in?'

Maestro Fantin had spotted her in the mirror and gave her one of his special smiles, which doubled the number of wrinkles on his old face. 'Zoe, how lovely to see you. How are you?'

Zoe went into the room and gave him a deep bow, the kind that boys do, with one arm behind her back and the other reaching down to almost touch the floor.

'I'm fine,' she said. 'Did you have a good holiday?'

'It was a holiday for old people,' he said, with a smaller smile. 'You know, those health spas, they're like dinosaur cemeteries. All those people walking around really slowly. You watch everyone moping around the corridors and the park and then you realise that if you're there, then you're just the same as them, and that's not a pleasant thought. I'm always happy to get back here. You're so beautiful, you young people. Just seeing you makes me feel better.'

'Is that why you keep on playing the piano here even though you could stay at home?' The words just slipped out of Zoe's mouth before she'd realised they were there.

Maestro Fantin wasn't at all offended. In fact, he laughed – a low and gentle chuckle. 'Yes, that's why. Even though I have to say that at my age I'm a bit fed up of the same old Mozart all the time.'

He played the first few notes of the tune that he always used to accompany their *pliés*, then rounded it off with a cheerful arpeggio. 'Some Rachmaninov would be a bit more like it, eh?' And he started playing the gloomy, mysterious music that he'd been playing just before. It was the sort of music that made your hair all messy when you played it, thought Zoe, as she watched

Maestro Fantin's long white locks tremble and bounce and fall in front of his eyes.

'That music's so . . . full of passion,' Zoe said when he'd finished and the long chord full of echoes had slowly died away. 'It's like the soundtrack of one of those big movies, the sort that's full of tragedy and makes you cry your eyes out.'

'It has the same effect if you're playing it. It stirs up all sorts of emotions inside you,' replied Maestro Fantin. 'Like when you're watching a storm or one of those spectacular sunsets with huge, puffy clouds in all different colours. Would you like to dance a thunderstorm?'

Zoe wasn't dressed for dancing. She was wearing jeans and her basketball shoes, but she kicked off her shoes and tugged off her socks, so her feet were bare. Just like that, she went and stood in the centre of the room and signalled to Maestro Fantin that she was ready and he started at the beginning again.

How do you dance a storm? Zoe couldn't explain it. You felt agitated inside, furious, frightened, all at the same time, and when the thunder came it felt like one thousand hearts beating at once. You jumped, then you curled up on the ground, then leaped up, up, up, to touch the grey sky, catching hold of a flash of lightning and flinging it at something ugly, something that needed to be destroyed . . . maybe one of your own fears. Then the roaring grew quieter, even though there was still the occasional dull rumble of thunder in the distance, and a great feeling of calm descended upon everything, your movements slowed down, became more relaxed, and you just wanted to stop and rest, maybe even fall asleep. At the end of her dance, Zoe stretched out on the floor, face down, arms out, and for the third time in just a few minutes she listened to the echoes of the final chords fading away.

'Well, that was fun,' said Maestro Fantin when it was over.

'Yes, it was,' Zoe agreed. She sat up and crawled over to get her socks and basketball shoes, and then put them back on. Then she stood up and did another bow. 'Maestro Fantin, goodbye and thank you,' she said, in a solemn voice.

He stood up with a little difficulty, then pressed his hands down on the keys. What came out this time wasn't a magnificent chord, but a muddle of sounds. 'This is my farewell to you,' he said. 'It seems appropriate, after a thunderstorm.'

There was another person Zoe hadn't seen for a while, so she wolfed down her food and mineral water at lunchtime, said goodbye to the others, helped herself to an apple from the dessert tray and bit into it as she walked away. 'Where did you say you were going?' Leda shouted after her, over the din of mouths munching away and talking at the same time. But Zoe was too far away to answer without yelling.

Demetra never ate in the school dining hall. 'It would ruin my stomach,' she said. Instead, she brought in a proper meal from home to eat. 'Come in, come in,' she said when she saw Zoe standing in the doorway of the costume department, and she waved her in. She'd cleared the big wooden table, which was always covered with material and half-finished costumes, so that she could eat her lunch. She'd pushed back the fabrics so that they wouldn't get dirty, but the table top still showed traces of their presence: the odd sequin flashing in the sunlight, pieces of silver and gold thread, a pin with a red head and a pin with a blue head.

As Demetra slid her salad and cheese on to her fork and ate her lunch, Zoe sat on a high stool and looked around. The costume department was a fascinating place, a sort of cabinet of wonders from which anything might appear – like that bird-of-paradise costume, for instance, that was dangling from a clothes hanger, covered with scraps of fabric to imitate the blue feathers of a peacock or the green plumage of a humming bird. Or like the dark-blue cloak embroidered with gold moons, suns and stars, which was probably designed to conceal a fairy of the night.

As Zoe inspected all of the new costumes, Demetra

finished her lunch. She closed the lid of her electric-blue lunchbox, wrapped her fork in a paper napkin and put everything into a bag, which she then popped on to the floor and pushed beneath the table with a foot that was wearing a comfortable tartan slipper. She cleaned her hands with a hand-wipe that gave off a nice, fresh scent, then pushed her hair back and gave a deep sigh. 'A bit of relaxation always does you good,' she said. 'Particularly at the moment, with all those Movit devils around.'

'Didn't they bring their own costumes with them?'

'Yes, of course they did. But there are always some little repairs to do, or a costume that's too tight and needs to be let out a bit, or one that needs to be taken in at the waist. And some of the materials they use in America aren't that easy to sew, so it's really hard work.'

'You know Lucas is in their show, don't you?' Zoe said to her.

'Of course I do,' Demetra answered. 'But don't ask me to show you his costume. I'm making it because they didn't come up with the idea of having a boy in the show until they started rehearsing. They didn't know anything about it when they were devising the choreography or they'd have brought a costume with them. Anyway, it's a surprise.'

Zoe gave Demetra a knowing look of affection. Demetra was one of the pillars of the Academy. She'd been working there for thirty years, since the time, she always said, when she didn't even know how to thread a needle, even though Zoe had her doubts about that ever having been the case. Demetra was bound to have been a brilliant costume-maker even as a girl. Now she headed a team of four, and she was the only one to have a workroom all to herself. The others were all together on the other side of a glass door that opened only when Demetra said so, and that didn't happen very often. 'Because sewing is an art,' Demetra always said, 'and every art has its secrets.' Looking at the things that Demetra was able to make, Zoe was more than convinced about that.

'So, my little star, something to tell me?' Demetra asked her, sinking into a comfy armchair with flowers on, which looked more like something you'd find in a living room than in a sewing workshop.

'I'm missing Madame Olenska a bit. That's funny, isn't it? I should be happy. Gimenez is a lot less strict and she gets us to do fun stuff that we've never done before. But I don't know . . . something doesn't seem right. I hope Madame's enjoying herself.'

'Well, I don't know if she'll be enjoying herself as such. Her mum's very old and she's not well. That's the main reason she went. And I think that everything will have changed a lot since she left. You set off with all of your memories intact and then the reality wipes them all out, even though they say that St Petersburg's a really beautiful city and it could only have got better in recent years. Some of those rich Russians *really* are rich,' said Demetra, rubbing her thumb and fingers together.

'But Madame Olenska can't have been very rich. She left home with just one suitcase.'

'And how do you know about that?'

'Er, I heard her talking to Maestro Fantin one day,' Zoe admitted.

'So you had your ears open when they should have been closed, eh?' Demetra pursed her lips and gave Zoe a stern look.

'No, no,' Zoe protested. 'I was just going past her office and the door was open. I walked straight past. That was all I heard.'

'I know. You're not the type to spy on people,' said Demetra gently. 'Not like that nasty little piece of work in your class, that Laila.'

Zoe realised that Demetra was about to make one of her revelations. The costume department was a magnet, attracting all of the gossip about what was going on at the school. So as not to spoil the suspense, Zoe said nothing, but just waited, fidgeting a little on her stool. Laila had been unusually quiet for a while. She hadn't been showing off. She hadn't been making mean jokes about the abilities of the rest of the class. In fact, Zoe had barely noticed that she was there. For someone who thought she was the most brilliant ballerina at the

Academy, she really wasn't doing much to stand out.

'You know what Laila's done this time?' Demetra said, after a dramatic pause.

Zoe shook her head.

'She went to Gimenez and told her that Alissa had serious problems. An eating disorder, she said. And she told her that ill people shouldn't be allowed to study at the Academy, because they create a bad atmosphere and prevent everyone else from concentrating on their work.'

Zoe shuddered. Even for Laila, that was a really mean thing to say. Even if it was true that Alissa had had some problems, it was obvious to everyone that it was all in the past. You only had to see how enthusiastic she was about the lessons to know where her focus was.

'Who told you that?' she asked Demetra.

'Gimenez. She came to talk to me because she knows that I've been here for ages and I know everyone. That's what she said.'

'And?'

'Well, I told her that I didn't know anything about Alissa and this business with eating disorders or whatever, which is true, but that I do know that Laila's a snooty little busybody who's only happy when she's making other people miserable.'

'And what did she say?'

'She said it was a shame that a girl who was so gifted didn't have a character that matched her talent. I like that Gimenez. She's really great – and the way she dresses is so elegant, so unusual. You should see the way the other teachers look at her.'

Zoe laughed. Yes, she'd already noticed that. They were all jealous of her.

'They're jealous.' Now that she'd said it out loud, it seemed perfectly obvious. 'And Laila's jealous of Alissa too. But why? I mean, Laila's got everything she wants. She doesn't need to say mean things about other people.'

'It's not a question of needing to, sweetheart. She just can't help herself. It's like having a vicious little creature inside you, gnawing away at your heart. In the end, you're full of holes and all of the good things escape and instead of a heart you've just got a kind of dried-up old conker all riddled with holes. Then you're all on your own.'

'You're right. Laila is all on her own,' Zoe remarked. 'She doesn't have any friends. She's always with her mum and dad outside school.'

'They're probably fed up with her as well. Or maybe they're just the same as her. She must have got that bitterness from someone, mustn't she? Anyway, sweetheart, I'd better get back to work now. Be a good girl and go back to your friends. You've still got five minutes before classes start.'

Zoe left Demetra with a strange sensation of anxiety. She'd gone to see her expecting to feel better when she left, the way she always did when she visited Demetra, but instead she just felt a bit queasy, as if the lunch she'd just eaten had been too much (but it was only a small portion) or hard to digest (but it had only been pasta). What could she do to get rid of that anxious feeling that had taken hold of her and was stopping her from thinking of anything else? Well, nothing at the moment, because she had to go to her English class. And, fortunately, after that it was character dance. Maybe that would do her some good.

That evening, on the bus home, Zoe was looking out of the window, daydreaming away, when she felt a hand on her shoulder. She whipped around, a little frightened. The touch of the hand almost felt painful. On the bus, you were amongst strangers, people who didn't have the right to come that close to you. But then she recognised the owner of the hand, and she smiled. It was Roz, who used to live in the same street as Zoe when she was little. She had moved house when they were both seven, but before that they'd been inseparable for a long time. It had been nice, going from one house to the other, just four doors down, without even having to put on your coat.

'Hi,' said Roz. She didn't seem to have changed at all. She still had the same light-blue eyes, wavy blond hair the colour of straw, fair skin, and soft, plump cheeks. Zoe wondered if she still looked the same to Roz.

'Are you coming home from school?' she asked her.

'No, sax lessons,' Roz answered, pointing at the rectangular bag hanging from her shoulder.

'I didn't know you played,' said Zoe.

'Of course you didn't. We haven't seen each other for ages,' Roz said, but her tone was gentle. She was just stating a fact, perhaps with a touch of sadness. 'You're on your way home from the Academy, aren't you?'

'Yes.'

'How are things going?'

'Fine,' Zoe answered. Then, with a sudden burst of honesty, she said, 'Actually, I'm not sure. I'm fine, but not all of the people in my class are that great. In fact, some of them are a real pain.'

'You get that wherever you go,' Roz said, nodding. 'Just ignore them, and make sure you choose the right people to spend time with.'

'I know. You're right. But what if the wrong people are being mean to the right people?'

As she was talking, Zoe found herself thinking how easy it was to be honest with a person you felt comfortable with, even if you hadn't seen them for ages. That was a nice thought and it cheered her up a bit.

'Well, I suppose you have to do something about it.'

'But what would that be? What if the wrong people are so wrong that you know that talking to them won't do any good?'

'Then you'll just have to bump them off,' said Roz. Zoe's eyes widened, but Roz laughed.

'I'm joking, of course. It's just my way of saying that there isn't any alternative. If you've got a problem, you have to face up to it and talk about it. It's not a good idea to pretend there's nothing going on. The problems are there and they're not going to solve themselves.'

'We should meet up sometime,' said Zoe, abruptly changing the subject because they were getting close to her stop. 'When are you free?'

'Wednesdays and Thursdays after school. Give me a call,' Roz said, and Zoe got off the bus and waved as it left the stop.

Face up to your problems. Talk about them. It sounded easy. But how exactly did you do it?

CHAPTER EIGHT

It's Not Easy Being Small

'Zoe, go and get Maria, would you? She's been shut away in her room for an hour. She's probably wearing headphones and can't hear me. I've already tried to call her several times. I've got to pop down the road and fetch some books I left with a neighbour, but when I get back I want us all to sit down and eat. Give Sara a yell too, while you're there.'

Her mum was leaning against the doorframe, tugging on her shoes. She seemed quite distracted. She was always so busy, with this and that.

'If you want, I'll go and get them,' Zoe offered.

'No, you know I don't like you going out alone when it's dark,' her mum said, disappearing through the door. A moment later, Zoe heard the thud of the front door closing. With a sigh, she put down the book she'd been reading (*The Best Love Poems of All Time* – such a beautiful book!) and headed for Maria's room.

She knocked, even though it felt a bit silly knocking on a six-year-old's bedroom door, but it was important to respect people. Then, as no one answered, she turned the door handle.

As her mum had suspected, Maria was immersed in a wash of silent music, with the CD player lying on the bed beside her and the headphones in her ears. She was sitting with her legs crossed. The strange thing was her expression – it was empty, miles away, as if she were enchanted or entranced, staring at something that she couldn't comprehend. It was a strange expression to see on a little girl's face.

Zoe stood in front of her, waving her hands like one of those men in orange jackets who guide aeroplanes on the runway. Maria tugged off the headphones and looked Zoe up and down. 'What is it?'

'Dinner's ready. We'll be eating in five minutes,' Zoe said to her.

'I'm not eating anything,' Maria replied.

'What do you mean, you're not eating anything?'

'I'm not hungry. When you've got a lot of things to

think about, you can't waste time eating. And anyway, I've got a knot where my tummy should be.'

'Can I sit down?' Zoe waited for a nod and then sat down on the edge of the bed. She held her arm out and Maria immediately snuggled up beneath it, as if that was what she'd been waiting for.

'So, do you want to tell me what you've been thinking about?'

'Julia says she doesn't want to be my friend any more.'

Julia had been Maria's friend since their first year at nursery. They did everything together. They'd even managed to end up in the same class now they were at primary school. It was impossible to imagine them separated or angry with each other because they were both such nice little girls. The two of them were cheerful, friendly, full of sweetness and light.

'Why not?'

'She says I'm boring and that she wants to be Cho's friend instead. They're always together. They've swapped friendship bracelets. They play together at breaktime. They hold hands when they go to lunch. I'm left all on my own.'

'But Julia's not the only person in the class, is she?'

'No, but I only want to play with them if Julia's with me.'

'Aren't you friends with Cho?'

'She's one of the ones I only want to play with if Julia's

there. She's Chinese and she's got beautiful hair. It's really black and straight, and she wears these unusual hair bobbles in all kinds of different colours. Julia started saying that she had the most beautiful hair in the world and that she really wanted to have hair bobbles like that as well, because they were so different from the normal ones that you get at the usual shops, and so Cho brought in a whole bag for her as a present because her parents have a shop that sells that kind of thing, and ever since then Julia's spent all of her time with her and she won't even look at me. We still sit together in class, but that's it. And she won't even look at me when I'm sitting next to her. She faces in the other direction and puts her pencil case on the desk as a barrier. That's just mean, isn't it?'

Zoe thought about it for a while before answering. 'I don't know if it's mean. If you ask me, she's just a bit confused because she thinks that friendship means that you have to be friends with one person at a time. But that's not true. You can be friends with lots of people because we're all different and you'll like something about one person and something else about another person. Like me, for example. I'm friends with Leda, but I'm friends with Alissa and Lucas too.'

'And with Roberto,' added Maria, seriously.

'And with Roberto,' Zoe agreed. 'Listen. I think this is what you should do. Go to Cho and ask her if she wants to be friends with you. Is she nice?'

'I think so.'

'Then it'll be easy. She'll say yes and then you'll be friends and Julia will understand that all three of you can be friends, and you'll have much more fun.'

There was another thud – the front door closing. Mum must be back. 'Girls,' their mum called. 'Are you still hiding away? When are you going to come to the table?'

'Shall we go?' Zoe said. Maria was still huddled up to Zoe. She felt soft and floppy, like a rag doll.

She looked up at Zoe and said, 'Your plan sounds a bit silly to me. I mean, do you really think it'll be that easy?'

'Try it,' Zoe said to her. 'Then if I'm wrong, come and tell me and we'll come up with another idea.'

'You can come up with another idea. I still can't think of anything that will work,' Maria said, but she was obviously feeling a bit less upset now. She even managed to produce a little smile. 'Wonder what Mum's made for dinner,' she said, sliding off the bed.

'Let's go and find out,' Zoe answered, taking her by the hand.

At school the next day, Zoe asked to leave the classroom and go to the toilet. She didn't actually need to go, but she went anyway, because that was where she'd said she was going. She really just wanted to be on her own for a few minutes. DT classes were so dull. What with the teacher saying boring things in a very deep voice and everyone muttering away in the background, it just resulted in a kind of low buzzing sound that was enough to send anyone to sleep.

She washed her hands. As she dried them on a paper towel, bits of it stuck to her fingers. She rolled the wet paper up into balls and brushed them off. Then she looked at herself in the mirror. Her face was pale and her freckles stood out as if they'd been drawn on with a pencil.

Then she heard a tiny rustling sound behind her, and a small noise, like the whimper of a frightened animal. She turned around. Sitting on the floor, with her knees pulled up to her chest, was a little girl. It was one of the second year juniors, and with a little effort Zoe even managed to remember what her name was: Robyn. She was staring straight ahead and sobbing without properly crying, quietly, with a little shake of her shoulders.

Zoe knelt down in front of her. 'What's the matter, Robyn?' she said, in the kindest voice she could summon.

At first the little girl didn't answer. Zoe put a hand on her head and gently stroked her hair, the way you do when you're trying not to frighten a baby animal. 'Will you tell me?'

'Only if you don't tell anyone else,' the little girl answered between sobs.

Zoe drew a cross over her heart. 'Cross my heart,' she said.

'I stole Francesca's trading cards,' she confessed, and those strange sobs without tears became faster. 'A whole pile of them. *Hello Kitty* cards. I took them from her pencil case when the others were out in the playground. She told the teacher that she couldn't find them and the teacher said that whoever had taken them had to own up, otherwise she'd punish all of us and we wouldn't be allowed to play outside for a week. Everyone except for Francesca, but who's she going to play with if no one else is allowed out?'

'You should go and tell your teacher that it was you,' said Zoe. 'That seems like the best idea.'

'But if I tell her, Francesca won't want to be my friend.'

'That may be true, but how can you carry on playing with her as though nothing's happened? You know that it was you who took her cards. You'll feel really bad. It will be like having a stone in your heart. Do you know what I mean?'

The little girl just nodded and finally a tear, one single tear, rolled down, along her straight little nose.

'Your teacher will find a way to sort it all out, you'll see, but you have to tell her right now. The longer you keep that stone in your heart, the more it'll hurt.'

'I'm not sure I can do it,' said the little girl.

'You'll never know if you don't try. Come on. Stand up,' said Zoe, rising to her feet and holding her hand out to help the little girl. Robyn took hold of Zoe's hand and, once she was on her feet, carefully brushed herself down, and wiped her dusty hands on her trousers.

They left the toilets together, blinking as they went back into the bright light of the corridor. 'Go on,' said Zoe, giving her a gentle nudge. The little girl started walking. She still had the softly bouncing, puppet-like walk that small children often have. Zoe watched her all the way back to her classroom. Then she sighed, and went back to her own classroom to be bored for a little bit longer.

That afternoon, she had just managed to get the front door open when Maria dived into her arms the way she usually did with their dad when he got home in the evening. There was something different about her, and it took Zoe a moment to realise what it was. Instead of wearing her hair loose, the way she usually did, she had it up in four wacky bunches that made her look a bit like a doll. 'Look at my bobbles,' she said, turning her head this way and that so that Zoe could see them properly. In her hair, she was wearing a cluster of small translucent spheres, a piglet's face with black beads for eyes, a chubby little star with pink liquid and a cloud of sequins inside, and a kind of blue crystal with lots of facets and edges. They were indeed very unusual bobbles.

'Cho gave them to me. We're friends now. Me and Cho,' Maria explained.

'What about Julia?'

'Oh, I don't know. She's upset because Cho played with me all day today and she gave me these presents. She'll get over it though,' said Maria, with a shrug of her shoulders.

Zoe felt like laughing, but managed not to. Instead she said, 'So, yesterday you were miserable and today Julia's miserable.'

'I don't care,' said Maria, folding her arms. But just a moment later she squinted up at Zoe and added, 'Well, I do care a bit, but not much. She started it.'

'That's true. But now you've got a new friend and Julia's upset.'

Maria sighed. 'What should I do?'

'Well, you could try phoning her. You know, just to find out how she's doing.'

'Maybe I could pretend I'm phoning to say that I didn't make a note of what page of the book we were supposed to look at for tomorrow,' said Maria.

'That sounds like a good idea. Go on then,' Zoe said to her, and she watched as Maria skipped away to use the phone.

The next time Zoe saw Robyn was on the stairs at school. Robyn hadn't noticed her, because she was much shorter than Zoe, and she just kept on going. Zoe stood in front of her. 'Hi, Robyn,' she said. 'Is everything okay?'

'Hmm,' was the response. Was that yes or no?

'What does "hmm" mean?' asked Zoe.

The little girl lifted up her face, looked into Zoe's eyes, gave a deep sigh and said, 'I told the teacher and I gave the cards to her. The teacher said that as it was the first time I'd done such a mean thing she wasn't going to tell anyone. She gave the cards back to Francesca and told her that the cleaner had found them. So now Francesca has her cards back and everything's fine.'

'Is it?'

'No, not really. I still did a mean thing. So I was thinking that maybe it would be better to tell Francesca, and then I wouldn't feel so bad about it. You know, to get rid of that stone in my heart that you were talking about.'

'I'd think about it for a bit longer, if you're not sure.'

'Okay,' said the little girl and she skipped away as though she were feeling lighter already.

In the toilets, standing in front of the mirror again, still pale, still with too many freckles, Zoe laughed. What was she turning into? An agony aunt for little girls? Did she really know the right thing to say to them? Then she answered her own question. When someone asks you for help, you do what you can. The real help is just listening.

But then she thought of Laila and Alissa. What happened when you were the one who needed to do something?

CHAPTER NINE

A Beast of the Forests

'So how are the rehearsals going?' asked Zoe, as she, Leda and Lucas went up the stairs to their next lesson.

Lucas pulled a mysterious and happy face and put a finger to his lips. 'Top secret.'

'Is it a secret that you have to keep or a secret that you want to keep?'

'I want to.'

'Can't you just show me even one step, just a short sequence?'

'No, absolutely not. I want it to be a surprise for everyone.'

'Do you know how mean you are?' said Leda.

Lucas just stuck his tongue out at her and said, 'Yes.'

Zoe laughed. 'Well, at least that's something.'

Although the rehearsals with Movit and their angels were veiled in the utmost secrecy, Lucas made no secret of his desire to dance and the real joy that it gave him.

In Kai's character dance lessons, they were studying some sequences of a famous dance by the Ballets Russes. They were all sitting in a relaxed circle, with their teacher Kai at the centre, talking and waving his arms around enthusiastically.

'It's called *L'après-midi d'un faune*, and it's based on music by Debussy,' said Kai. 'It was first danced in Paris in the 1910s, where it caused a huge scandal, but was also a great success. It starred a sensational dancer and choreographer called Vaslav Nijinsky. Have any of you heard of him?'

Lucas's hand shot up. 'I've seen photos of him.'

'Can you tell us what you remember, what struck you about the photographs?'

'Well . . . he was like some kind of animal.'

Everyone laughed. Kai moved his hands like the conductor of an orchestra does, to quieten them down, and said, 'No, no. There's nothing to laugh about. You're absolutely right, Lucas. A faun is a mythical creature of the forests, a wild creature, who acts according to his passions.'

'Nijinsky had these patches all over his costume,'

continued Lucas, 'almost like leaves or bits of fur perhaps, but it wasn't the costume that really made you think he was a wild animal – it was the look in his eyes. It was his body too, the way he was standing. He looked nothing like a classical ballet dancer. He wasn't standing there with a nice, polite smile on his face. It looked as though he'd been surprised just as he was about to leap. He looked like a carnivore, some kind of predator.'

No one was laughing now, because Lucas was so wrapped up in what he was saying. He was speaking with such passion and moving his hands as if he could actually see this strange beast of the forests standing there in front of him.

'That's exactly right.' Kai stood up and went over to press a button on the projector and the picture that Lucas had described appeared on the back wall of the room, up above the mirrors. He had a wild expression with eyes wide open, showing the whites on all sides, and an angular body, paralysed in a position that was almost unnatural. He was wearing such a very strange costume. 'There's a short film too. Ignore the speed – it's an old film. Just concentrate on the way he moves.'

A fragment of a silent film came to life on the wall. Old films usually made you want to laugh. The people move in such a jerky way, and too quickly – whatever they're doing – so that it always looks like one of those old slapstick movies. But not this time. There was so much passion in those tense leaps, in those flashing knees and elbows, in the strange angle of the head. It was hard to define this animal, even though you knew that it was a faun. What was a faun? Had anyone ever seen one? It had something of a snake about it, and the gracefulness of a deer, and the twitchiness of a reptile, all at the same time. Zoe watched, enchanted, knowing that she would never manage to do anything even remotely similar. Then, when the film finished, she looked over at Lucas whose face was lit up, entranced. He could do it. He could learn to dance like that.

When Kai played Debussy's music for them (that was strange too) and asked who wanted to try dancing to it, Lucas *was* the first to jump to his feet.

Everyone watched Lucas, fascinated by what he would do next. It was as though he'd tried, and tried again, until he'd achieved the kind of imperfect perfection that the part required. Lucas was the faun. Now it was perfectly clear what kind of creature the faun was. He was a cautious animal waking up from a sleep that hadn't been as calm as it looked. How could you sleep calmly in the forest when your enemy might attack at any moment? Then he was suddenly up on his feet, looking around suspiciously, ready to leap away at any strange sound. He seemed to be the prey, but then he became the predator, the lord of the forests, moving silently amongst trees, proud, alive, full of pent-up energy. How was he going to free that energy? By running? Hunting? Killing? Who could say?

When the music finished and Lucas dropped to the floor, exhausted by the intensity of the dance, loud, spontaneous applause broke out. Kai clapped with the rest of them. 'Bravo, Lucas. A wonderful re-enactment of the myth of Nijinsky.'

'It was great,' he said, with a big grin on his face. 'I felt so free.'

'That's all part of dancing,' Kai said, very seriously. 'Feeling free. Conveying the idea of freedom. Having your own body under complete control, yet managing to communicate a sense of freedom.'

As they were going back to the changing room, Zoe found herself behind Leo and Matthew. Leo was muttering away, practically into Matthew's ear, '. . . throws himself around like an idiot, and the teacher actually praises him for it! Anyone could dance like that.'

Zoe couldn't contain herself. She put a hand on Leo's shoulder. 'Is that right?' she said to him, when he turned around with a look of surprise on his face. 'So why didn't you do it then, if you think it's so easy, if anyone can dance like that?'

Leo's face crumpled, his sneer giving way to astonishment. Zoe caught a wry grin from Matthew out of the corner of her eye. Then she walked past them and ran down the stairs. She wanted to jump down the last five steps, but that was against school rules. It really was very important to have complete control over your own body, wasn't it?

'Do you fancy going to the cinema?' Zoe asked Lucas.

It was raining. It was March and there didn't seem to be much else to do in the rain-soaked city.

'What's on?'

'There's a special showing of *Finding Neverland* this week,' Zoe casually suggested.

'Boooring! Peter Pan!' said Lucas. 'The boy who wouldn't grow up. What a load of rubbish. I can't wait to grow up.'

'Why?' Leda asked. 'So that you can buy yourself all the PlayStation games you want?'

'That's one reason,' Lucas grinned. 'But mainly to find out what's going to happen to me.'

'I'm fine with *Finding Neverland*. It's got Johnny Depp in it – an angel in human form,' sighed Leda.

'It's fine by me too,' Roberto said. 'Not because of Johnny Depp, but because of *Peter Pan*. It's my favourite book.'

'So it's three to one,' Zoe concluded happily.

The film was sad and a little bit strange. It was about a lonely journalist, the author of *Peter Pan*, who fell in love with an entire family that wasn't his own, but then later on they did kind of become his family. Zoe had read an article that said that in real life the man virtually abandoned the children that he had loved so much – who he'd practically adopted and made into characters in his books – and when he died, after becoming rich and famous, he didn't leave his money to them, but to Great Ormond Street Hospital in London.

The best thing about the film were the games that the writer and the children played together. It was always nice to see a grown-up playing with a child as an equal. Zoe thought about her own dad. Obviously he didn't play with her any more, but he still played with Maria a lot and, even though she couldn't remember all of the details, she knew that he used to play with her too when she was the right age. Their favourite game was Noah's Ark, because they got to pretend to be all of the animals going into the ark in pairs, with all the right sounds and actions.

It wasn't as though Zoe missed being small, but she wasn't in as much of a hurry to grow up as Lucas was. At the moment, she liked things as they were. Some days and weeks seemed to flash by like lightning, but others just dawdled and hung around like a bunch of sloths. Time was a strange thing. For Zoe, now was the time to spend with friends, especially with Roberto. As she had that thought, she took his hand and he turned his head to look at her and smiled, before going back to concentrating on the film. The light of the big screen danced over his face. Roberto was so handsome. Or was she the only one who saw him that way? It didn't really matter. All that mattered was being together and feeling so good that you didn't want to be anywhere else.

Afterwards, they went to a bookshop. Leda disappeared into the children's section, looking for a teen romance novel. Lucas went off to the travel department – his parents wanted to take him to Kenya in the Easter holidays, but he preferred the idea of Florida and was trying to persuade them to go there. Zoe stood in the theatre section, leafing through a big book full of photos and posters from the Ballets Russes. It was too expensive for her to buy, but she was happy to look through it and commit to memory those beautiful ballerinas' eyes with their dramatic make-up and the bizarre, innovative costumes. Kai had explained about the scandal that the Ballets Russes had caused in Paris. Even though the city was full of art and excitement at that time, anything that was too new could still cause a commotion.

'Come and look at this,' Roberto called to her from the next set of shelves. She left the book open at a portrait of Nijinsky and went over to Roberto. The book that he showed her was called *Pavlova*. The information on the cover said that she'd been a great dancer in the early twentieth century and that she'd left Russia to live in America and had made ballet popular all over the world. Zoe was pleased about that. It was good to hear that a woman had the skill and the opportunity to create a bit of a commotion as well.

'Wasn't she beautiful?' Roberto said to her and showed her a photo. The face was very intense, and very sweet.

'It says that Roland Petit has paid homage to Anna Pavlova with a ballet called *Ma Pavlova* – My Pavlova,' Roberto said. 'Maybe it'll come to the Academy one day and we can go and see it.'

'You're really interested in this kind of thing, aren't you?' Zoe asked him, without taking her eyes off the ballerina's intense face. 'What I mean is, you're not like Lucas. He puts his heart and soul into what he's doing. But you're different. You seem to take a step back from everything. It's as though you're always thinking really hard about what you're doing.'

'The truth is that I still haven't decided what I want to do when I grow up. I think I might like to be a choreographer instead of a dancer. You know, coming up with ideas, creating stories for people to dance.'

'So that's why you're so interested in books?'

'Books, films, photos, going to see shows. That kind of thing. What about you? What do you want to do when you're older?'

They'd never talked about it before, and Zoe was a bit

surprised that it had come up this way, almost by chance, standing there amongst the books and the other people, beneath the bright, harsh lighting, instead of in the half-light under the trees in the park, for example, sitting close together on a bench.

She thought for a moment. 'I don't know. I mean, obviously I hope to become a proper ballerina. I'm one of those girls who fell in love with the tutu and the pink slippers when I was about four,' she confided. 'We're all quite similar. I suppose it's rather dull really. There are far too many of us. Natural selection will take us out, one by one, year after year. Sometimes I feel lucky that I'm still at the Academy, but then sometimes it feels like a burden, because you have to work so hard to stay there. Dance is still what I enjoy doing best, though I'm not certain that it'll always be like that. I'm not like Laila.'

'Laila? Mmm, that's a great example. If she becomes a prima ballerina or a soloist, she'll be one of those complete divas who float around with their noses in the air.'

'She seems to think that you don't have to be nice as long as you're successful.'

'But success doesn't bring you happiness. It's like money. Or so they say. I wouldn't really know,' Roberto said with a grin.

'Ah, you might not be rich, but at least you're good-looking,' Zoe joked, and then she blushed, because she'd never paid him such a direct compliment before. He looked deep into her eyes.

And then the moment was gone, because Leda turned up, grinning with excitement and clutching a book with a bright pink sparkly cover. 'Look! *All American Girl 2* is out!'

As she hadn't read number one, Zoe didn't know quite what to say, so she just nodded. Then Lucas turned up as well, holding a guide to Uruguay. 'I've changed my mind,' he announced. 'I want to go to Montevideo.'

'Why?' Roberto asked him.

'Anywhere with "video" in the name sounds like my kind of place,' said Lucas, and they laughed.

'Have you made sure that spring isn't the monsoon season in Uruguay?' Leda asked.

'Monsoons? Do you actually know where Uruguay is?' Lucas asked her, smiling.

'No idea. It sounds really exotic and faraway though . . . Why are you all looking at me like that?'

Sometimes things happen when you're least expecting them, when you haven't predicted them, when you're not ready. One afternoon, by some strange coincidence, Zoe looked around the changing rooms after lessons had finished and realised that all of her classmates had gone. All except one. Laila was still there, slowly putting her clothes away in her locker. This was her chance. Almost before she knew what she was doing, Zoe found herself standing in front of her. Laila pretended she hadn't seen her and just carried on carefully winding the long ribbons round the soft pink shoes.

'Hey,' said Zoe, and it came out almost as a snarl. She was surprised to hear how low and tense her voice sounded, how laced with fury.

'What is it?' said Laila, in her usual whine, without even looking at Zoe.

'Turn around and look at me. I've got something to say to you.'

'Let's hear it then.' She gave Zoe a sulky stare and pouted. With the bun in her hair still perfect even after all the exertions of the lesson, her cheeks gently glowing with two rosy circles, and her big blue eyes wide open, she looked like a mechanical doll or a ballerina in a children's story. She was simply despicable, Zoe thought. She actually felt as though she detested her at that moment, and she put all of her anger, passion and disdain into what she was about to say. Her words came out smoothly, easily, as though she'd prepared what she was going to say, but that wasn't the case at all. It was her instinct that was speaking, a kind of furious instinct to put things right, to restore justice where there was none.

'I know that you've been saying mean things about Alissa. You've been saying that people who are ill like her shouldn't be at the Academy. I don't know what it was that possessed you to say something like that, but I promise you that if I find out you've done it again . . .'

'What are you going to do? Hit me? You know the rules. You'll get expelled. Anyway, that idiot Alissa has signed her own death warrant. Do you think that Madame Olenska will want an invalid in the class when she gets back?'

'Alissa isn't an invalid. She's made a really good recovery.'

'She keeps locking herself away in the toilets. I've seen her. Who knows what she's up to in there? It's exactly the way she was last year.'

'So why should I believe you? All that comes out of your mouth is lies and spitefulness.'

'You know what? You're an idiot too. Don't you see that it makes sense to eliminate the competition? The fewer of us there are, the easier it is to succeed. It's that simple. It's natural selection. We'll be studying it in science at some point. It's a law of nature – the best succeed, while the rest just fall away. It's the way things are, whether you like it or not.'

'Yes, but natural selection has to happen by itself, not thanks to the intervention of a poisonous witch like you.'

'A poisonous witch? I've never been called that before. I'll take it as a compliment. Now get out of my way. I'm leaving.'

It had been years since Zoe had last felt like hitting

someone. That had been when she was about five and there was a boy at the park who kept stealing her plastic racquet. One time he'd even taken it home with him. Then the next day he pretended it was his and that it always had been. Zoe pulled it from his hand and whacked him on the head with it. Someone had stopped her after the third whack. Now Zoe really felt like hitting someone again. With a racquet, with her bare hands, maybe even scratching with her nails as well. But she stopped herself and it wasn't because of the school rules, it was because she knew that it wouldn't solve anything. It would just be playing Laila's game. Laila stood up, humming to show she didn't care, threw her soft pink leather bag over her shoulder (her mum and dad had bought it in Paris for her to keep her dance things in – there wasn't a person in the school who didn't know about it) and walked away.

The next day, after lunch, Zoe made sure that she was on her own with Alissa. She'd watched her at lunchtime and Alissa had eaten up every single thing. She'd chosen healthy, simple food and hardly paid any attention to what was on her plate, because she was so wrapped up in a discussion with Leda about American teen romances, which were better than those from anywhere else in the world. 'They're the most romantic romances of all,' Leda had declared.

Zoe had been following Alissa everywhere she went, but tried to be casual about it. Up the stairs they went, into the classroom to fetch a packet of tissues, and then down into the garden, to sit beneath the trees, chatting some of the time and spending some of the time in silence.

'I need to go to the loo,' Alissa said after a while.

'I'll come with you,' said Zoe, a little too quickly.

Alissa gave her a surprised look. They hadn't gone to the toilets together in pairs since the first year at school, but she didn't say anything. She just let Zoe tag along. When they reached the toilets, however, Zoe realised that playing detectives like this was ridiculous. 'I'll wait for you out here,' she said to Alissa. She leaned on the window ledge and looked down into the playground, watching her friends playing dodgeball, as always, and she felt stupid and dishonest. She was being so unfair, believing Laila's mean gossip about Alissa, but she had to find out whether it was true.

When Alissa came back, Zoe just blurted out, 'I'm sorry. Somebody said that you've been spending too much time in the toilets. I followed you because I wanted to make sure that you were okay. I don't have the right to spy on you. I want to know just one thing, and I want you to be the one to tell me: are you okay now?'

Alissa looked at her and smiled. 'You can answer that for yourself, can't you? Look at me. Do I look okay?'

It was only at that point that Zoe noticed the very

thin line of violet pencil around Alissa's eyes and the touch of pink powder glistening on her eyelids.

'Yes, you look great,' Zoe answered. Alissa smiled. 'And your make-up's so subtle that it should escape the eagle eyes of even the strictest teachers.'

'I'm not kidding myself. If Madame Olenska were here, she'd already have pounced on me by now, but it's different with Gimenez. She always wears so much make-up herself. I'm sure that she wouldn't even notice, as long as I'm sneaky enough and don't make myself look like a clown. I wear make-up because I want to look nice. And I want to look nice because there's a boy I like. It's that simple. I'm not going to the toilet to be sick, I come to the toilets to put on a little make-up to make myself feel better – and to go to the loo of course! You do believe me, don't you?' And Alissa raised an eyebrow and looked at Zoe with vague apprehension.

'Of course,' said Zoe. 'I really am sorry.'

'No problem. I understand that you were concerned about me, but you don't need to be. Honestly. If I think I fancy someone, that can only be a good thing, right?'

'Yes, I suppose so,' said Zoe, smiling. 'Even if you don't tell me who it is!' she teased.

They both giggled and went back down to the garden, with their arms around each other's waists like a couple of ballerinas dancing a duet.

CHAPTER TEN

Successes and Discoveries

Zoe thought the hubbub in the foyer of the Academy Theatre before a show was one of the most wonderful sounds in the world: people crowding towards the entrances, having their tickets checked by ushers who looked like highwaymen in their black tailcoats and white gloves. It all made her feel a little dazed. She imagined that it was how you might feel when you'd had a glass of champagne – it gave you a little sparkle inside. Zoe was dressed very elegantly, in a black miniskirt, a black sleeveless roll-neck top and the pink jacket that she'd bought when she went shopping with Alice when she'd visited a few months ago. She wasn't wearing any make-up. She'd tried some on, but she felt ridiculous, so in the end she wiped it all off with two cool pads soaked in rosewater. It felt so good that she almost wanted to put on lots of make-up, just so she could take it all off again.

'You've got big eyes already. If you wear make-up, they'll look even bigger and take up the whole of your face,' Sara had declared as she helped Zoe with her experiments. 'Take my advice and forget about the mascara as well. All you need is a bit of lip-gloss. You're so lucky.'

Roberto looked very stylish too, in a smart blue shirt, grey trousers and polished leather shoes. 'Very Italian,' commented Leda, who looked gorgeous in a short-sleeved black dress with a high collar. Her long legs looked even longer than usual in her tights, which had tiny white dots on. It felt strange, just the three of them being there without Lucas. However, even though there were only three of them, they were all there to see Lucas, so perhaps it wasn't really that strange after all. Zoe's dad had taken them to the theatre. It was the first time they'd gone to see a show by themselves. Of course, the Academy Theatre was so familiar to them that it almost felt like home, but it was still really exciting. They said hello to Alex, a friendly usher who was also in the top year at the school, and went in to find their seats in the stalls.

In the end, Leda's idea of going to see the afternoon performance hadn't worked out; they simply *had* to go to the premiere – they just couldn't wait until the Sunday.

In the orchestra pit, the musicians were tuning their instruments, and the trilling of the flute, the singing of the violin and the magical sound of the oboe joined with the bustle of the crowd, merging to create a growing sense of anticipation. Movit didn't usually work with an orchestra, but *Angels* was an unusual show for them, and they'd made a few changes. One change was that they weren't taking it on tour to the usual simple dance spaces, but to the really big traditional theatres instead. The music was an anthology of excerpts by great musicians, from Beethoven to Brahms and Stravinsky, the kind of pieces that orchestras usually have in their repertoire. Sitting in her seat, Zoe leafed through the programme, and her eyes fell upon the following tiny words: *The Young Angel – Lucas Sinise*. It really was him. Lucas.

Then the lights finally dimmed and the conductor came in, accompanied by the first burst of applause, and the curtain went up to reveal the black void of the stage. Zoe felt excited, tense, nervous, worried and happy, all at the same time.

They had to wait quite a long time before it was Lucas's moment. The choreography was absolutely sensational, even better than they'd anticipated. There were angels tumbling from the heavens, angels spreading their wings in mid-air, dirty metropolitan angels with feathers so covered in mud that they seemed unable to take off, and yet they still did, flying up into the air, light and free, ignoring the burden of their enormous wings. Of course, everyone knew the wings were made of foam rubber, but they seemed to have the consistency and radiance of clouds or candyfloss.

Zoe had long ago given up wondering what it all meant when she went to see contemporary dance. Sometimes it wasn't about telling a story, it was about conveying sequences of emotions. Everyone reacted differently to the cascade of ideas. There wasn't just one way to feel, one path to follow, but the effect was so powerful. When you watched these dancers, you believed that angels really did exist. You couldn't help but believe, and you thought that this was exactly what angels were like – black ones dressed in dazzling white, white ones dressed in oily black, simple, sublime beings sweeping the heavens with their flight.

Then the Young Angel finally made his entrance, and there was Lucas, standing on the stage in front of them. He came on with a spectacular pirouette. His wings were smaller than the adult angels' wings and were very close to his back, so he was free to make beautiful movements, leaps and somersaults. The young angel had a specific role – taking souls by the hand and comforting them, leading them from one world to the next. You saw him soothing them, coaxing them, making them laugh and cry. Then he took them along with him, tugging them with all the insistence of a child who wants to show you his favourite toy. The world to which they were transported really was just like a huge toy, a brightly coloured marvel, where black and white dissolved and all the different shades of colour mixed together. It was a new life. It was a beautiful life.

Zoe had tears in her eyes, but without the usual knot in her throat or in her stomach. This was pure happiness, but it was overflowing and it had to find some way out, so it transformed into hot drops, which rolled down her cheeks and ended up in her nose. Zoe thought that it was a mystery why tears always ended up in your nose. In films, hardly anyone ever sniffed when they cried. But you had to in real life. So Zoe sniffed as quietly as she could for a while, and then there was nothing to cry about because Lucas had left the stage with a triple cartwheel and his part was obviously over. But at the end, he came out for the bows with all of his distinguished companions, and when he did a forward roll and leaped up and bowed, the crowd went wild. Zoe suddenly spotted Lucas's mum and dad in a box. They were absolutely radiant, and clapping so hard that it looked as though their hands were about to drop off.

'I really liked the choreography,' Roberto whispered in her ear. 'I'm not quite sure why. I've still got to think about it, but I definitely liked it.'

'One day you'll choreograph something even better,' Zoe replied. 'Maybe even something for me.'

Going to the dressing rooms to say hello to the dancers was another of the many pleasures of an evening at the theatre. Zoe, Roberto and Leda knew all of the secret passages, the doors cut into the velvet or covered with big pieces of cloth, so they were able to take short cuts, and arrived a lot sooner than the crowd of fans who were determined to get autographs from their favourite dancers. They even got there before Lucas's family.

As he was the only boy in the show, he had the privilege of a dressing room all to himself, and it felt strange, but nice, to see his name on the door. They didn't even need to knock. Lucas opened the door as they arrived. He'd obviously been waiting for them. He'd taken off his wings and hung them up out of the way, because they were so fragile, as wings always are, but he was still wearing his white shoes and his white costume. It was looking a bit less white now – there was always a lot of dirt on the stage. Zoe assumed that he must have at least two costumes because there was another performance on Sunday. Imagine if you washed it and it didn't dry in time! What would you do? Use a hairdryer? His black skin looked so black against all of that white, and his eyes and his smile looked really bright too. It was quite a contrast. Even under the harsh neon lighting (why didn't they put better lighting in the dressing rooms?), their friend seemed to be glowing, as if he was lit up from inside, like a light bulb, transparent with happiness and pride.

'I've got a present for you,' said Leda. This surprised everyone because they hadn't talked about it before. Zoe hadn't thought of buying anything for Lucas and it was obvious from Roberto's expression that the idea hadn't occurred to him either. Leda dug around in her black rucksack and pulled out a toy bear with two sweet little gold wings sewn on to its back. 'I know that it's not quite as elegant as one of those Movit dancers, but it was the closest thing to you that I could find,' she said, waving it in front of Lucas's face.

He laughed as he took it from her and then made it hop up and down on the palm of his hand and said, 'Thank you, he's really cute. I don't know how much he'll enjoy being in my bedroom, but I'm sure I'll find a place for him.'

There was a knock at the door. It was Lucas's family. His mum had her arms around a huge bouquet of white flowers, which she immediately handed over to the artiste, giving him a big hug at the same time. Her words of affection were lost in the crackling of cellophane. Then it was his dad's turn, and this time the flowers, which were still in Lucas's hands, were in serious danger. Zoe swiftly rescued them, and smoothed out the crinkled wrapping and bouquet. Flowers for a boy? wondered Zoe. Well, why not?

Monday morning at school was complete chaos. Everyone who loved contemporary dance or was at least vaguely interested in it – and that meant half the school – wanted to congratulate Lucas. Even the older boys stopped and crowded round him. Zoe couldn't even see Lucas in the crowd, but she knew he must be the centre of that circle in the middle of the corridor, which was so big and dense that it was difficult to get past. It was as if a street artist had decided to put on a show there and had immediately drawn a huge crowd of spectators. Zoe squeezed through between the wall and the outer reaches of the circle and just managed to catch a few words above the babble of voices. 'They did everything. I just had to listen and do what they told me to.' Typical Lucas. As if it was easy to listen and carry out instructions so perfectly, like a real professional, especially when it was one of the most famous dance companies in the world and you'd never danced a step with them before. As if it were the most natural thing in the world.

But for Lucas it probably was the most natural thing in the world, Zoe thought as she went into the classroom. Roberto was already at his desk and he waved at her. She walked over to him and smiled, but her eyes were drawn to an object he was wearing around his neck

– a surfer-style pendant that was so out of character for him that it almost made Zoe laugh. A lot of the boys had recently started wearing stuff like that. If he'd been dressed the way he had at the premiere, the pendant would have looked ridiculous, but he'd chosen to wear a T-shirt and a hooded top and jeans, so it didn't look too out of place.

'It wasn't true, was it?' Zoe said to him, without taking her eyes from his pendant.

'What wasn't true?'

'Come on, Roberto. Fess up. What you said about having an allergy. If you were allergic to rubber you couldn't wear that thing around your neck,' and she reached out to touch the black rubber cord that the pendant was hanging from. 'You just pretended you couldn't wear the rubber costume so that the part would go to Lucas.'

Roberto pulled a face, looked out of the window, and shrugged his shoulders, all at the same time. He turned to Zoe and said, 'So? I was interested in it, but not completely passionate about it. Sure, I was happy when they picked me, but it wasn't the most important thing in my life. I don't want to be a Movit dancer when I grow up. Lucas does. Besides, he was so close to getting the part. There was just a whisker between us, they said. Anyway, I think they made a mistake. I mean, they picked me, but he was really the right person for the job. Auditions are always like that. They're so short and you have to give it your very best shot, so you end up feeling too tense and you don't make it. I wasn't the slightest bit nervous, so everything went really well for me. Lucas was all wound up and full of expectations and that's probably why he didn't dance as well as he usually does, and it was the one time when he really would have wanted to do his very best. So, I just told a little lie. One little white lie. You see?'

As he took off the rubber cord and hid it in his pocket, Zoe looked at him affectionately. She'd never heard him make a speech like that before, partly because he was a boy of few words, and partly because even though he spoke English well, he had quite a strong Italian accent, and occasionally he still stumbled over a word or pronounced something incorrectly. It was actually really sweet. What he'd done for Lucas was sweet as well. So, without even thinking about it, Zoe took his hands, pulled him up and gave him a big hug.

'You two! Have you forgotten that this is a classroom?'

The sharp voice of their English teacher brought them straight back down to earth. They pulled away from each other and turned to look at her, but they immediately saw that she wasn't really angry. She just thought it was amusing.

Zoe slinked away to her own seat, Roberto sat back down, and the classroom slowly filled. It was just a normal day. A day after a fantastic show. You can be doing all kinds of really normal, everyday things, but, with a precious thought in your heart, even the everyday stuff can become a little magical.

CHAPTER ELEVEN

The Return
of Madame Olenska

It was Monday. A very special Monday, because it was the day Madame Olenska was returning to the school. Zoe went up the stairs with a vague feeling of apprehension and sensed an almost imperceptible change in the atmosphere. Everybody was moving more quietly, more calmly. There was no running and no yelling.

There she was, at the top of the second flight of stairs, leaning on her usual cane. Madame Olenska's fearsome walking sticks, which she used to beat out rhythm and which she always seemed ready to fling at the head of anyone who wasn't doing what they were supposed to be doing, were as simple and unadorned as you could imagine – as black and shiny as gun barrels, with no metal tip or handle. Once you'd got to know her, you could picture her holding a cane with a knob in the shape of a dragon's head, or a medusa, or a chimera, or some other terrifying mythical beast. But her canes weren't like that. It was their simplicity that made them so frightening.

Today Madame Olenska was actually using the cane to lean on, not brandishing it about like a weapon. She seemed fragile. She seemed really . . . old. She wasn't really, really old, of course, but she must have been about sixty. Zoe had worked it out once by putting together the few details of her biography that she knew. Three months in Russia, far away from the world of dance, must have taken their toll.

The children walked past her and greeted her. 'Good morning,' she said to each of them, one by one, giving them a penetrating stare and a nod of the head.

Then it was Zoe's turn. 'Good morning, Madame Olenska,' she said. 'Welcome back.' She expected a simple nod in return, but Madame held out her cane in front of her and put her free hand under Zoe's chin.

'Is everything all right, Zoe?'

'Everything's fine, Madame,' Zoe answered. She wasn't frightened. The headmistress hadn't frightened her for a long time now. If anything, she was slightly bewildered, as were her classmates, who stood staring at the strange scene for just a little too long and then hurried away when their desire not to become involved in Madame's business became stronger than their curiosity.

Then the moment passed. Zoe walked away, still feeling the touch of those cold fingers on the skin of her face. She had answered with complete honesty: everything's fine, Madame. Because now that Madame Olenska was back, Zoe was sure that everything would indeed be fine. There was no place for stupid gossiping when Madame Olenska was around. With her, there was only justice, a justice that was so exact that it gave you a real sense of calm, if you were in the right. If you were in the wrong, however, you'd probably tremble with fear at the mere thought that she might find out one day and you might just end up giving yourself away for that very reason.

Zoe felt calm as she went into the classroom that Monday. She really liked Gimenez and had acquired something of a taste for freedom during the weeks she'd been teaching. Even the barre could mean freedom, once you'd completely mastered it. It wasn't just about mindless repetition of the exercises which were always the same, from when you were little until you were the biggest star of all. No. It was the simplest way to free your body, to give it all that it needed in order to perform what you asked of it.

Estelle and Stephanie were muttering in a corner. 'So the fun's all over now then,' said Estelle.

'Now that she's back we're going to have to behave,' agreed Stephanie.

'No more make-up. Bye bye, lip-gloss.'

'It was so much fun when she was away.'

'We'll be little old ladies before she gets round to taking another holiday.'

Zoe didn't agree with a single word of what they were saying, but she was careful not to say so. They wouldn't understand. They'd just call her a creep and say that she wanted to be Madame's pet. That wasn't true, but it wasn't something that Zoe could explain.

That afternoon, in the barre session, they were both there – Gimenez, dazzling in red and black, and Madame, all in black, looking very severe. Seeing them together like that, you couldn't fail to notice the difference between the two stages of life. Gimenez was in the prime of life, with her firm and rounded body – almost too firm and rounded for a ballerina – and a healthy energy evident in every position she assumed. Madame Olenska was mature, streamlined and pure, in both her body and in her gestures. Zoe looked from one to the other and didn't know which she preferred. Then she realised: she liked them both in different ways. She wanted to go and stand beside them to represent a third possibility, the stage of life that she was in herself – a girl who was still growing up, but who had the same deep and undeniable passion as the two women. Of course, she knew where her place was and she stayed put. At the end of the lesson, Madame Olenska banged her cane on the floor to get everyone's attention.

'I've seen for myself that your time with Gimenez has been productive, as I knew it would be,' she said. 'She is an outstanding teacher and an outstanding dancer. So, I have decided that she will remain with us. She will be my assistant in our dance classes. You will have two teachers instead of one, so I will expect even more of you.'

A laugh would have been appropriate at that point, just to lighten the atmosphere, but of course no one dared. There was perfect silence.

'As you've made such good progress, I think we can start your first exercises in *pointe* work a few months early,' Madame Olenska added. At that, despite the atmosphere of nervous respect, a happy murmur spread throughout the room. Going *en pointe* early? Learning to dance on the very tips of their toes at the end of this school year, instead of having to wait until next autumn? No one could have expected that. It was really big news! That was what every young ballerina thought about, from the very first day – wearing proper ballerina's shoes, made out of layers of cloth and glue with a toe box. They were usually terribly disappointed when they discovered that they'd have such a long time to wait.

Of course, this didn't apply to the boys. Madame continued, 'As for the boys, while we're learning to dance *en pointe*, they'll have additional character dance lessons.'

'While we're learning to dance *en pointe*.' Zoe savoured the words one by one and the one she liked best, apart from '*en pointe*', of course, was 'we'. Obviously Madame Olenska had been dancing *en pointe* for years, and so had Gimenez, but this was something important that they were going to be doing together.

'I'm happy that you're not just a substitute now,' Zoe said to Gimenez as she left the room.

'Me too,' she answered. 'I think we're going to do great things together.'

Zoe nodded, gave her a little curtsey and walked on. It must be horrible being a substitute teacher, she thought – you weren't a person in your own right. You were just filling a hole left by someone else. Then that person came back and you weren't needed any more. Gimenez was too strong, too good, to be just a stop-gap. It was great that things had turned out the way they had. What Gimenez had said was true, she could feel it – they were going to do great things, all of them together.

Afterwards, in the changing rooms, the usual everyday

chatter was swept aside by an explosion of exclamations, squeals and laughs. 'Isn't it amazing! I've never heard of a class being allowed to go *en pointe* so early. That must mean we're really good . . .' Francine twittered.

'I wouldn't be so sure about that "we", if I were you. I think the natural selection's about to begin,' Laila was muttering, but everyone still heard her, and they all ignored her.

'It's really going to hurt,' said Paula, always a realist. 'It hurts everyone.'

'Not girls who have a special talent,' replied Laila.

'We'll see,' said Anna, cutting her short. 'We'll see.'

But no one felt like arguing with Laila. Some of the girls had already switched on their phones and were calling home with the good news, where there were mums who knew very well how much it meant to be allowed to dance *en pointe*, even if they'd never done it themselves.

'She's not expecting too much of you, is she?' Zoe's mum said at dinner, when Zoe made the official announcement. 'You're rather young to be dancing *en pointe*, aren't you?'

'Yes, but all of the girls are very well trained,' Sara said, suddenly seeming like an expert on classical dance.

'And they wouldn't take any risks at the Academy, would they?' her dad said. 'I mean, they're not going to push anyone too fast.'

'Of course not,' Sara said. 'If anyone is too slow for them, they'll just throw them out.'

She sneaked a glance at Zoe, who just smiled and said, 'I'm not worried. We'll take things one step at a time. We've got two fantastic teachers,' and she told them that Gimenez was going to be staying.

'So what do you think that means?' her mum wondered. 'Do you think Madame's feeling under the weather?'

'No,' said Zoe, defending her. 'It's just that she always has so much to do that she really needed an assistant.'

'I really can't imagine Madame Olenska feeling under the weather,' her dad said. 'Dance is her life. The Academy is her life.'

'I wonder if it's enough for her,' her mum commented. 'Does she want anything more? Has she ever had other hopes and dreams?'

'Well, she's had a really interesting life,' her dad replied. 'America, and all those tours . . . She hasn't always been a teacher. She's been around the world.'

'Will you stop talking about Madame for a while? I'm going to be dancing *en pointe*, for goodness' sake,' Zoe shouted, and she surprised herself with the strength of her feelings.

Her mum and dad burst out laughing, followed by Sara and, a moment later, by Maria.

'Oh, of course. Our little star needs to be in the

spotlight,' her dad said. He stood up, took hold of the lamp that was hanging above the table and shone it into Zoe's eyes. 'Would you please tell us how it feels to be dancing *en pointe*? It must be such an extraordinary experience.'

Zoe shielded her eyes with her hands, laughing, and replied, 'No comment.'

'Quite right,' her mum said. 'We'll talk about it again when it's time.'

CHAPTER TWELVE

A Saturday Afternoon in Springtime

It was a Saturday afternoon in springtime, one of the best kind, with a warm sun and a blue sky. It felt wonderful after so many wintry Saturday afternoons spent inside cinemas or shops, trying to escape the cold and the rain. On a Saturday afternoon in springtime you could just go to the park and stay there all afternoon, which is what Zoe and her friends had decided to do. You could do whatever you wanted, as long as you prepared properly. Lucas had brought a ball, which had taken up all the space in his rucksack. Roberto had a frisbee with him. The girls had just brought themselves

– they were dressed in comfortable clothes, trainers and tracksuit bottoms, because, just for once, they didn't feel like being perfectly dressed little madams going for a walk through the town centre. Even Leda, who always paid so much attention to the way she looked, wanted to be free and relaxed.

After a wild game of football and then throwing the frisbee around, everyone had felt a bit tired so they'd decided to go to the café by the lake. The waitress had just brought them four absolutely magnificent ice cream sundaes, decorated with little umbrellas and with flags stuck into the top. They were piled so high that they looked a bit precarious. There was silence for a while, the exquisite silence of people who are eating something delicious and don't want to be disturbed. Then, when most of the ice cream had been demolished and the rest could be sucked up with a straw because the ice cream had melted, they could start talking again.

'Let's give Alissa a call,' Zoe suddenly suggested.

Leda looked at her. 'You're right. We should have thought of it before.' She already had her mobile in her hand and was selecting the number from the list. She pressed another button. 'Alissa? Yes, it's me. We're at the park. Me and Zoe and the boys. At the café by the lake. Are you doing anything? Well, why don't you come and join us then? We'll wait for you. Yes. Bye.'

She got there in fifteen minutes, running the whole

way. Out of breath, she dropped on to a seat beside them. 'What shall I order? A big ice cream like yours?' she asked, looking at the liquid remains in the glass dishes. A couple of minutes later she was demolishing a chocolate sundae with great determination. It was topped with a happy explosion of sparkling strands on a stick that looked like something off a Christmas tree.

'You're always together, the four of you,' she said when she'd finished, leaning against the back of the chair.

'You've got some chocolate round your mouth,' Lucas pointed out. Alissa licked all around her lips until she found it.

'There can be five of us if you like,' Roberto said. 'Leda and Lucas aren't a couple, so it's not as if you'd be getting in the way.'

Zoe blushed and hoped that no one would notice and that the others were all looking elsewhere. If Leda and Lucas weren't a couple, then Roberto obviously thought that he and Zoe were. Hearing him say it made her feel a bit funny. Was it nice? Yes, it was a sort of tingling sensation – but with a bitter aftertaste, as if people who weren't part of a couple should be less happy somehow. But then Zoe cheered up. Leda and Lucas seemed to be perfectly content as they were, and Alissa was obviously comfortable with them as well. So, if they were all happy, why should she start wondering why and how and if it was right and if it would last?

Sometimes Zoe thought she'd like to spend less time thinking about things, and just to accept things as they were. Thinking sometimes gave her too many ideas. One thing just led to the next, and she never knew where she was going to end up. Take Laila and her spitefulness, for example. She started by thinking about her and then ended up thinking that she'd like to eliminate her from her mind and from her life and from the lives of all the people she hurt, as if she were a virus. The trouble was that Laila's nastiness made Zoe feel nasty too – after all, Zoe had said very unpleasant things about Laila. But maybe even the Lailas of this world had a purpose. Perhaps they were there so that you could understand how you *didn't* want to be, how you *didn't* want to behave. They were there so that you could learn how to defend yourself from them, to protect yourself, to act as though nothing was the matter. And if you succeeded, you realise that the Lailas of this world could be dangerous, but ultimately they ended up damaging themselves more than anyone else – they were all alone.

Did she really not feel at all sorry for Laila? Perhaps not. At that moment, Zoe wanted to be generous, but she knew that it was just because she was having a nice time. She was enjoying a beautiful spring afternoon with her friends and with her . . . hmm, with Roberto, and everything seemed to be right with the world. So maybe she could allow herself a little bit of compassion for monsters, and have some sympathy for their deep, solitary sadness. But Zoe couldn't feel anything positive for Laila, even though she tried really hard. She was disappointed with herself. She would have liked to feel more magnanimous, to hold out a hand to Laila as she had to Alissa, with the same natural ease, but she knew that it was too late for that. Perhaps that was what growing up meant — choosing your battles, deciding which side you were on. You couldn't always sit on the fence. It just made you confused and it didn't solve anything.

It was at that precise moment that Zoe, who was really happy as she was, suddenly realised that she wanted to grow up as well — to grow up and to find out what was waiting for her around the corner. If she stood on her tiptoes, trying out those *pointe* shoes she'd been wanting for so long, would she be able to see better? Would she be able to see further? Who could say? Zoe only knew that it was a beautiful Saturday afternoon and that a Monday full of exciting new things was waiting for her. She had something to look forward to and even the waiting felt wonderful. It was packed with all kinds of dreams and desires and possibilities.